Wolf's Blessing

The Shifter Brotherhood, Volume 1

Blake R. Wolfe

Published by Blake R. Wolfe, 2023.

This is a work of fiction. Similarities to real people, places, or events are entirely coincidental.

WOLF'S BLESSING

First edition. June 8, 2023.

Copyright © 2023 Blake R. Wolfe.

ISBN: 979-8223832737

Written by Blake R. Wolfe.

One: Ronan

I slammed a handful of silver coins down on the counter, blood smearing across the surface of my fingertips.

"I need a room, food, a bath, and some company for the night," I said, staring the tavern owner down.

"Right away, sir," he said, scooping the coins off the counter. He paid no mind to the blood. Reaching down, he grabbed an iron key from below the counter. "End of the hallway on your left," he said, pointing to a door at the back of the tavern. "I'll have the bath filled right away."

"Good," I grumbled, heading that way.

"Sir?"

I stopped, turning back to face him.

"About your company... What is your preference?"

"Male," I grunted, rolling my bulging muscular shoulders. "Someone that can handle getting fucked."

"Right. Sorry for holding you up, sir."

The truth was, I'd probably fuck anyone that let me right now. After two weeks filled with death and slaughter, I was too tense and worked up to be picky. My last job had taken me far away from home, leaving me stranded in the most godforsaken city in all of Eadronem, Terrastera. It was home to nothing but poor miners and sycophants looking for a nobleman to suck off to get ahead. There wasn't anything for me there, and probably no jobs either. Thankfully the previous job paid well... perhaps because I was the only survivor. It turns out bandits can be clever when they want to be, and the rest of my group had been subdued in a matter of moments. But me? Well, I had a secret, which was the only reason I was still alive.

And for now, it would remain a secret. Once I was back with the Brotherhood, I could be myself again. But in places like Terrastera, where those bastard clerics wandered the streets day and night looking for people to turn in for clout or coin? It was the last place anyone wanted to get caught being different.

Different got you killed in Eadronem. Especially when you were close to those fucking religious zealots. Of course, the nobles were no better. They'd chew you up and spit you out before you knew what was happening. But thankfully, they kept to Aratis, the city floating high above Terrastera, casting it in near-permanent darkness. It was held there by the massive crystal that hovered between the two cities, or at least that's what people said. They claimed it was the source of all magic and mankind's link to the gods.

I thought they were full of shit.

Sure, there were a handful of people who could do magic. But most were corrupt officials, nobles, or greedy assholes worshiping the crown. Except for a couple of mushroom-addled druids, I'd never met a magic user that wanted to do any *real* good in the world. Then again, I guess I couldn't blame them. The world was pretty much shit already. No amount of magic was going to make it better.

Besides, it wasn't like I was doing any good either. If mercenary work didn't pay, I wouldn't be doing it. Hunting monsters and bringing in bounties wasn't my idea of a great life, but I made a decent living. It got me out and about to several different places in the world, something most people never even dreamed of doing. The people of Terrastera were far too poor to worry about seeing the world, especially when their meals were spaced so far apart. Mining was the only real work in that wretched town; from what I'd heard, it wasn't going well. I pitied them, but that's as far as it went. No single person could save their failing industry. They'd either adapt or die. That was the way of the world.

But none of that mattered right now. I only wanted to get out of my sweaty armor and into a hot bath. After that, I'd dick down whomever they sent me and drift into a restless sleep. The moon was only a week away from being full, and I could feel the pull of its power in my blood.

However, the wolf would have to stay hidden until I could get out of town, which I planned to do in the morning. I didn't want to risk an accidental shift and end up in prison for the rest of my life. Not many people looked kindly on shifters, especially werewolves. They thought our disease was contagious. And they were right. Some did change after being bitten. It was how I became one. But most of them died, the wolf consuming them from the inside out before they could adapt to its power.

It was probably better that way. The world already had enough monsters, and most wore humanoid faces. Not that anyone would admit that. They liked to blame their problems on anyone but themselves.

I charged down the hall, already undoing the leather straps holding my armor on. My breastplate slipped off just as I reached the door. Throwing it open, I tossed the metal down on the side table, scaring the attendant that was inside filling the bathtub. But I paid her no mind, continuing to undo the straps on my pauldrons, unlacing my gauntlets, and removing the shin guards strapped around my legs. I had stripped out of my clothing by the time she finished filling the tub. Kicking my boots to the side, I turned toward the bath, not caring that I was completely naked. I stank, and my wolf senses made that even more evident. Not that the attendant seemed to care. She was taking her sweet time getting an eyeful of my body.

I stopped short of the tub, staring at her with one hand on my hip. Sweat mixed with old blood and dirt dripped down my body, but it didn't seem to faze her. I knew she'd never seen a man like me, and I relished the attention. Werewolves tended to be handsome, muscular, and well-endowed, something many other people in Eadronem were not. Well, except for maybe the Orcs, they didn't often come into big towns like Terrastera. I knew I was a rare sight with my deeply tanned skin, thick dark chest hair, and a dick that had made more than one concubine walk funny for a week.

"You're in my way," I said in a low growl. I leaned down closer to her. "And you're not my type. Move it."

She shook her head and bowed quickly, nearly sprinting out of the room. Her quick exit made me chuckle, and I turned my attention back to the bath. It was a smaller tub than I wanted, but it would have to do. That was the problem with being a big and robust wolf. Everything was too damn small. However, the water was still steaming, and I wouldn't waste it.

I had only just sat down in the hot water when there was a knock at my door.

"What?!" I called out, annoyed that someone was bothering me already.

I heard the door crack open slowly behind me. "Your company for the evening, sir," a baritone voice said.

"Come in," I sighed, resting my head against the tub's edge.

The door creaked as it pushed open behind me. I heard it close, followed by the sound of footsteps. A moment later, a figure stood beside the tub, blocking the light of the fireplace against the wall. I glanced up at the man that looked to be in his early twenties. He was thin with light hair and brown eyes, gazing downward at the ground. I noticed his clothes were tattered, and a fresh bruise bloomed under his left eye with a small cut just below it. I had a feeling I already knew where he'd gotten it from.

"Anything I can help with, sir?" he asked, quiet and timid.

I leaned forward in the tub, grabbing the cloth hanging over the edge and handing it to him. "I can't get my back."

"Of course, sir," he replied.

It was a lie, but I needed to ask him a few questions before we got to business. Taking the cloth, the man knelt behind me, wetted the fabric, and began to run it over my shoulders. His hands felt shaky and weak as he attempted to scrub the evidence of my last job off my skin.

"What's your name," I asked gruffly.

"Leif," the man replied timidly.

"My name's Ronan," I replied, rolling my shoulders slightly. "How long do I get you for tonight, Leif?"

I felt the man wince, the cloth stopping for a second. "I usually provide service for an hour."

"An hour?!" I turned to face him, meeting his brown eyes for the first time. "That's not going to be nearly enough. I'll need you until sunrise."

"I'm not sure if–"

"Will an additional gold piece cover it?"

Leif visibly shrank, his shoulders drooping as he nodded. "Yes, sir."

"Good."

At that exact moment, there was a knock at the door.

"Come in!" I called.

The same woman that had filled my bath entered the room, balancing a tray with meats, cheeses, bread, and a steaming bowl of stew. In her other hand, she held a large tankard, foam slopping over the side as she placed it on the small table in the corner. She made to leave, but I held up my hand.

"Hold it," I said, turning to Leif. I placed a thick hand on his shoulder, pulling him close. "When was the last time you had a decent meal?"

He looked over at the tray, his eyes full of hunger and desperation. "I... I'm fine."

That was answer enough. I turned back to the woman, pointing to my bag on the bed. "Take two gold pieces from that bag and show them to me."

She nodded, making her way across the room. I watched her closely as she rifled through the bag, pulling out the heavy coin purse I'd recently filled. Placing it in plain sight, she reached in and produced two gold coins from within.

"Good. Now bring me another meal and the person who ordered services from Leif. If your boss has a problem with it, tell him there's another gold waiting for him if he does what I say."

She darted out of the room with a slight curtsey, clutching the coins to her chest. I ignored the puzzled look from Leif and leaned back against the lip of the tub. Closing my eyes, I leaned back, enjoying the heat seeping into my pores.

"You aren't washing," I stated.

I could almost hear Leif shake himself out of it as he doubled down on scrubbing. He kept at my shoulders, working the rough cloth down my chest and torso before returning to my arms. Before he could get much further, there was a commotion outside my door.

"I'm sorry, sir, but this gentleman wishes to speak with you," the tavern owner said.

"I don't wanna talk to no one," a gruff voice returned, clearly on his way to being piss drunk. "Ain't nobody here worth my time."

"I assure you, sir, this is important."

"Who the fuck does this guy think he is?! What kind of tavern you runnin' here?!"

The door creaked open as the tavern owner entered. Leif stood up and backed away toward the wall, a look of fear on his face as the second man entered. He'd barely taken two steps into the room, and I could already smell the stench of booze wafting off him. I could also smell Leif's scent on him and the blood he'd yet to wash off his knuckles.

"What the fuck do you want?" the drunk bellowed. "I ain't got time for bullshit!"

"No, but you have time to beat up innocent people," I replied, not looking up at him.

"The fuck you say?!"

"You heard me. Gotta have a pretty small dick to do shit like that."

My wolf senses picked up the sound of his heart rate nearly doubling, anger flooding his body. He was stomping across the floor instantly, taking my bait just like I'd planned. I heard his boot whizzing through the air as he aimed a kick at my head, but it was far too easy to dodge. The sound of metal colliding with leather wasn't enough to cover up the cracking of bone as he broke a toe on the tub's edge.

Chaos erupted in the room as he howled in pain, hopping up and down. The tavern owner was trying to calm him down while Leif shrank further into the corner. I calmly pushed myself out of the tub, stepping onto the cold wooden floor as water streamed down my body. Striding up to the drunkard, I grabbed him by the collar of his shirt and lifted him clean off the ground, his yelps stopping instantly.

"There's no need for tha–"

"Shut it," I growled toward the tavern owner. "You shouldn't have let an asshole like this into your tavern in the first place." I pulled the man close, his face suddenly white as he realized how much bigger and stronger I was than him. "Tiny dick fucks like this one like to beat up courtesans, make them feel inferior when in reality it's *you* that's inferior. It doesn't matter what you've got swinging between your legs if you're just some drunk piece of shit hurting people to get off."

I turned us away from the others, making sure that only the drunk could see me before I let my eyes flash gold, revealing my true nature to him. His face paled even further, and I felt his breath hitch. He knew he was looking into the eyes of a predator, one that could kill him with a simple swipe of the claws.

"Now listen to me," I growled. "You're going to leave here and go home. Sleep all this shit off, and tomorrow, you can start a new life, one that doesn't require you to beat up innocent people." I gently placed him on the floor, ensuring he had his footing. There was the tiniest flash of relief in his eyes as he stepped back. "Oh, and one more thing."

I reeled back and decked him in the face, lifting him clean off his feet before he crashed back to the floor.

"That's a taste of your own medicine, you prick."

The man cupped the side of his face as he scrambled out of the room. He slipped and fell more than once, crashing into the hallway wall before he darted out of the tavern and into the night.

"That was completely unnecessary!" the tavern owner cried. "I should have you thrown out!"

I turned to face him, towering head and shoulders above him. "But you won't," I said calmly, reaching back into my bag for another gold coin. "And you're going to promise that you won't be taking customers like that anymore, or I'll come back and give you the same fucking treatment."

The tavern owner's face flushed as he gulped loudly. I pushed the coin into his pocket and forced him into the hallway. Grabbing the door, I leaned forward.

"Leif is mine for the night. Tell the girl to bring the food, and don't bother me again until noon tomorrow."

With that, I slammed the door in his face.

Two: Dante

"Acolyte Dante," a deep voice said, rousing me from my meditation.

I shook my head, looking at the familiar cleric hovering over me. It was Ryker, one of the five master clerics of the Aratis Twilight Temple. He was a hulking man, more fat than muscle, with an authoritarian personality to match. He had long dark hair pulled back into a low ponytail, not a single hair out of place as usual. His beard was also perfectly groomed, slicked into a sharp point in front to give him an almost menacing look. He definitely wasn't one of my favorite people in the temple, but he was a Master who needed to be respected. After all, climbing rank in the temple was the will of the gods themselves. Who was I to question their choices?

"Yes, Master Ryker," I replied, bowing my head. "What can I help you with?"

"Come with me," he commanded.

Without missing a beat, he turned on his heel and began briskly walking down the hallway, his shoes echoing off the white marble floors. I pushed myself up from the cushion and jogged after him, trying to straighten the wrinkles out of my robes as I went. I wanted to ask what was happening but knew better than to ask questions. The Masters would reveal their intentions when the time was right, just like the gods. It wasn't my place to question, only to follow the path set before me.

A few minutes later, I found myself ushered into Master Ryker's private chambers. He crossed the room and sat at a massive wooden desk covered in ornate scrolling. I didn't sit but waited patiently with my hands folded before me for him to speak. He shuffled through papers, looking for something. I thought he would speak when he pulled out a sheet at last, but instead, he pulled out a quill and began writing. He did that for the next ten minutes, slowly working through a pile of paperwork until he sighed and placed the quill back in the inkwell. He must have sensed my impatience and was trying to teach me a valuable lesson.

"Acolyte Dante," he said at last, lacing his fingers over his belly and leaning back in the chair. "Are you familiar with the Baron An'Cleth?"

"Yes, sir," I replied with a slight nod. "I believe he's the–"

"He owns the crystal mines in Terrastera," Ryker said, cutting me off. "And a significant patron of the Twilight Temple. He not only donates crystal to the clerics for the teaching of magicks, but he also owns the airships that we use to gather other acolytes and bring them back to the temple."

"Yes, sir."

This time I was keeping my mouth shut. Ryker was not a man that liked to be interrupted.

"It seems that Baron An'Cleth has run into a bit of an issue. His miners, stupid as they are, broke into a natural cavern under Terrasterra. Because of their folly, monsters have been let loose into the mines and have killed several of his workers," Ryker sighed. "They're now refusing to work, and two mercenary groups have failed to clear the way."

"That's bad, sir," I offered, hoping it was the right thing to say.

"It is indeed. That is why Baron An'Cleth has reached out to the Twilight Temple and asked for assistance from the clerics." He pulled another piece of paper from the pile, grabbing his quill again. "And I've decided to assign you to lead the next mercenary force into the mines to ensure its success."

"M-me, sir?" I replied, not quite believing my ears. An opportunity to prove myself would go a long way toward moving up in the Temple. Not to mention make me known amongst the nobles.

"Yes, you," he said. "The other Masters and I believe you are ready for this kind of mission. You've been with us for several years, and your magic is strong. We believe you could be a valuable asset to the Temple if you are applied correctly."

"Th-Thank you, sir," I stammered. "I won't l-let you d-down!"

"I'm sure you won't." Ryker signed the paper and handed it over to me. "You're requested down in Terrastera in three days. Get yourself outfitted by the Temple Armorer and prepare yourself. The Baron will have an airship waiting to take you down."

"Thank you."

"And one more thing, Dante."

"Yes, sir?"

"This mission must succeed at all costs," he said, his eyes flashing. "Mercenaries are a dime a dozen, but this crystal is important. Necessary *sacrifices* must be made for the good of the many. Heal them, ensure they get the job done, but do *not* form attachments."

"Yes, sir," I replied. "I remember my training. Attachments are the root of all suffering."

He nodded. "Being trained and being tested are two different things. The world is full of temptation. Many acolytes have fallen prey to her wonders." He leaned forward, his hands laced on the desk. "Be sure you're not one of them."

"I won't fail you, sir."

"Good. See that you don't. Dismissed."

Calmly, I turned on my heel and stepped out of his office. Although, the moment the door was closed, I couldn't help but flail for joy, containing all the shouts within my chest. I'd been living with the Clerics since I was thirteen years old, training day after day to hone my magic in a desperate attempt to become a high-ranking member. Seven long years of grueling days had made me lose hope. I thought the Goddess of the Twilight had forsaken me or at least deemed me unworthy. However, it seemed like she was looking down on me at last! The Baron An'Cleth was one of the most essential nobles in Aratis. Without him, there would be no trade with the world below, and the nobles would lose many of the things they took for granted. Living on a floating island high in the sky was beautiful and peaceful, but there wasn't exactly room for crops and livestock.

This job could change the entire trajectory of my life. Getting in good with Ryker and the Baron would put my name on the lips of the most influential people in the world. And maybe, if I exceeded their expectations, I'd be promoted up from Acolyte to full Cleric. That would mean a room of my own, an actual salary, and the ability to leave the Temple for extended periods of time. It was my ticket out into the world of Eadronem. Once I was out there among the people, I could do some real good at last. It was my fondest wish.

I nearly skipped back to the dormitory, drawing the gaze of more than a few of my fellow acolytes. It was odd for anyone to be outwardly emotional, but I couldn't help myself. I knew the goddess's teachings told us to keep our emotions in check, to be distant from the world so we could see it with eyes unclouded by sentimentality. Everything existed in the balance of light and dark, the twilight symbolizing the perfection of that balance. And yet, I still couldn't stop myself from being overwhelmed with joy. I hoped she'd forgive me for this one trespass on her teachings.

"You look happy," a voice said the moment I pulled the dormitory door closed behind me.

I glanced up, noticing my roommate and best friend, Calder, staring back at me. He was lying in bed, a thick leather tome with arcane symbols carved into the cover resting on his knees. Clearly, I'd interrupted him in the middle of studying.

"Is it that easy to tell?" I asked.

"You're practically glowing," he scoffed, snapping the book shut. "What happened to put you in such a good mood? One of the Masters faceplant in the fountain or something?"

"Don't say things like that!" I hissed, glancing around the room to make sure we were alone. It looked like our other two roommates were out, thankfully, because they were a lot less tolerant of Calder's jokes. "You never know who might be listening!"

"Whatever," he laughed, leaning back against the headboard. "Nobody likes the Masters anyway. They're all a bunch of pricks."

I sighed, rolling my head back to stare at the ceiling. There was no convincing him when he was like this. Calder was very set in his opinions, which I could understand. Unlike me, he actually had a family back home in Jyra, the one he'd been taken from when he showed signs of magical power as a child. Me on the other hand, I was just some orphan scrounging for scraps in the streets. Being picked up by the Clerics of the Twilight was the best thing that ever happened to me. Three meals a day and a warm bed were more than I could have ever hoped for.

"Master Ryker pulled me into his office this afternoon–"

"He's the *worst* one."

"He pulled me into his office this afternoon," I continued, ignoring his comments. "To offer me a job."

"Like what? Licking his fucking boots?"

"A job down in Terrastera for the Baron An'Cleth."

Calder's jaw dropped. "Get the fuck out…"

"No joke," I laughed, holding up my hands in mock defeat. "He wants me to lead a group of mercenaries to take care of a monster issue in one of the mines. From the way he talked, it seemed like a super important job."

"Sounds like a great way to earn the Baron's favor."

"Yeah," I nodded with a smirk. "That was my thought too."

"And you're gonna take it?"

"Master Ryker didn't really give me a choice." I saw Calder's eyebrow lift. "But I wouldn't turn it down anyway. I want the job. Anything to get out of this temple and breathe for a little while. I… I know we're not supposed to want things… but is it too much to ask to see a little bit of the world?"

"I don't think so."

Calder sat up, swinging his legs over the side of the bed as he tossed the book to the side. I stepped over to join him, sinking down on the lumpy mattress.

"I can't help but be a little trepidatious," I said, leaning against him. "But this'll be good for me. I'm... I'm determined to prove to them I'm worth something."

"You got this," he replied, nudging me on the shoulder. "You'll do a great job, and when you get back, you'll get promoted, and then you can sneak me some better food."

"You could get promoted, too," I said, glancing up at him. "If you wanted to."

"Nah, you know me. I'm too much of a loudmouth." He stared through the window over the clouds floating just below the city. "Everyone here knows I want to go home."

He was right, of course, everyone did know. For too many years as a child, he'd made his true opinions known. And now that we both knew it was better to be silent on such matters, the damage had already been done. Being near him also damaged my reputation, but I couldn't help it. Calder had helped me find my feet at the Temple of the Twilight. He'd been by my side since the first day I'd been brought in, and we'd been inseparable ever since. I loved him in a non-romantic way, even though it was against the teachings. I'd fought it for years, trying not to form an attachment to him, but to no avail. I figured if the goddess didn't want me to enjoy his company, she'd take him away. But there he was like always.

"So when do you leave?" Calder asked, shaking himself out of his thoughts.

"In three days. The Baron is sending an airship to take me down to the city."

"Well, make sure you pack an umbrella and a handkerchief," he sighed. "The nobles literally shit on Terrastera... and I can't imagine it smells terrific."

"Charming as ever," I sighed. "Thanks for the pep talk. I'm *really* excited to go now."

"I'm just telling it like it is," Calder shrugged. "Better to be prepared."

"Shit!" I said, hopping up from the bed. "I forgot to go to the armorer!"

Three: Ronan

I awoke just as the sun began to breach the horizon. The first rays of light filtered through the dirty window, striking the thin man lying beside me. He looked so delicate with the thin sheets draped over his naked body. The sun kissed his pale skin, and I wanted to reach out and touch him, running my coarse fingers over his body. But, true to my word, I hadn't touched him.

The night consisted of nothing more than a shared meal, some light conversation, and sleeping in the same bed since the floor was the only other option. Leif had told me a little about his life, but it was a story I'd heard a hundred times. He'd once been a boy without a home, skills, and nowhere to go. He stole to survive and eventually learned that sex earned more money than stealing. A few well-placed words and ten minutes later, he walked away with money to feed himself another day. Eventually, he found himself in Terrastera, and unfortunately for him, miners were a rough crowd. Between their gruff natures and the mines running dry, Leif found himself with fewer clients and more bruises; the frustration of the workers transferred to him.

He'd been slowly starving to death for weeks now. Another night or two and I may not have been able to help him. Thanks to my last job, I had enough spare gold to give him a better shot at life. Once he woke up, I'd send him on his way. There was a part of me, locked away deep inside that craved a relationship with someone like him. But I was part of the Brotherhood, and he was human. It could never work out. My life was a series of monsters and bounties, while his might turn out to be one of peace. He'd find a farm somewhere to settle down, have a family of his own, and live a happy life free from the horrors he'd seen in Terrastera. At least, that was my hope for him.

A life like that wasn't something I'd ever have. Werewolves didn't get happy endings. While the Brotherhood lent us some modicum of camaraderie, it wasn't a family. And that was my fate. I'd accepted it long ago.

Shaking my head to clear my thoughts, I tore my eyes away from the slight figure under the sheets and swung my legs out of the bed. The cold floor met my bare feet as I rubbed the sleep out of my eyes. It was another day, and that meant scouting for a new job. Once I sent the courtesan on his way, I'd need the money again. Maybe I couldn't have the kind of life I craved, but I could at least provide it to others.

I really needed to stop being so damn nice all the time. It was costing me a fortune.

Pushing myself up from the bed, I padded across the room and pulled open the door. There, lying in a neat pile, were my clothes that I'd had washed the night before. I gathered them up and went to the small table in the corner. There was a basin full of clean water, and after washing my face, I started to clean up the pieces of armor I'd stripped out of the night before. I scrubbed the dried blood and dirt out of every crevice as quietly as possible, trying to get some of the smell out. The worst part was the leather straps. No matter how many times I wiped them down, they just seemed to stink permanently. Eventually, I just pushed them aside. They were going to smell. That was the way of it.

As I pushed the last piece away, I heard a slight creak and looked up. Leif was sitting up in the bed; the sheets gathered around his waist as he watched me work.

"You're finally awake, I see," I said, tossing the dirty rag on the table. "Hopefully, you slept well."

Leif nodded, his eyes darting over my body. I glanced down, realizing I was sitting at the table, still completely naked. I wasn't a shy person by any means, but I didn't want him to think I required anything from him.

"Get dressed," I said. "You're leaving this tavern and this town. There's a new life waiting for you out there, one better than this."

His eyes widened. "But I don't have any money."

I crossed the room, grabbed my bag, and took out the sack of coins. Tossing it onto the bed, it spilled open, gold and silver coins scattering over the sheets.

"Looks like you've got money to me."

"I can't... this is too m–"

"No," I said, my voice firm. "You're going to take that money and make a better life for yourself. I won't have you sitting around here just waiting to get beat up again while you starve to death. Nobody deserves that."

He pulled the sheets aside, revealing his beautiful lithe form. His skin was so smooth, a trail of sandy blond hair running down his torso to a groomed tuft above his half-hard cock. I swallowed hard, looking him over hungrily. My own body began to respond, my dick thickening and beginning to rise.

"Can I at least repay you?" he said softly, his eyes glancing down to my pulsing shaft. "I'd be happy to do it."

I walked over, sitting down next to him on the bed. Taking a deep breath, I ignored every urge in my body to flip him over and fuck him right there until he was screaming my name. Instead, I reached my hands out, grabbing him by the shoulders.

"You don't have to do that anymore. That's all behind you now," I said, trying to keep my eyes trained on his. "The only thing you owe me is to go out there and make a good life for yourself. Nobody deserves how you've been treated here. Terrastera is a shit hole; find somewhere green and peaceful to live out your days."

"Are you certain?" he asked, leaning closer. "I don't know anything about you. How will I ever repay you?" He glanced down for a moment. "You... You could come with me...."

I stared into his brown eyes, fighting back the urge to kiss him. I kept reminding myself that I was there to help him. As much as I wanted a mate of my own, it couldn't be bought like this. If I took this man up on his offer and ran away with him, he'd spend the rest of his life thinking he owed me something. And because of that, I'd spend the rest of my life unsure if he actually cared for me or just felt indebted to me. That wasn't a life I wanted. No... we had to go our separate ways. Besides, I knew he wasn't the one I was looking for. He'd be easy to go with, but I'd never feel that deep sense of *connection* I was searching for.

"I'm afraid it'll be just you going on this journey," I replied. "Go find someone that makes you happy and start a life together." I stared at him for a moment. "But do me one favor."

He nodded. "Anything."

I closed my eyes, calling up the wolf inside me. The sudden wave of heat washed over my body, my heartbeat quickening in my chest. My nails elongated into claws, my canines grew, and my eyes tingled behind my lids. When I opened them again, I felt Leif tense under my touch, their true golden color on display for the first time.

"If you meet another like me, one of the Brotherhood," I said, my voice low and more gravelly than usual. "Treat them with kindness. We're not monsters, and an open mind isn't something we come across often."

Closing my eyes once more, all my features shrank back to their human form. I blinked a few times, the tingling sensation gone. In Leif's eyes, I could see my reflection returned to normal.

"Okay," he nodded, forcing himself to relax. "I promise."

He was still scared, and understandably so, but I couldn't blame him. It wasn't every day you came face to face with the terrors from children's stories and lived to tell the tale. Now, if I could convince a few more people that werewolves were decent, life would be much better for us all. But I knew, deep down, that would never happen. Too many wolves gave into their animalistic urges, hunting for the thrill of the kill. And most of the time, they found the most thrilling game to be people.

"Thank you," I said, patting him on the shoulder before standing up again.

I crossed the room, grabbed my clothes, and started to work them on. It took a moment to stuff my chubby cock into the fabric, trying to hide it the best I could. I could see Leif staring out of the corner of my vision, and it was only making things *harder*. Literally.

"Get dressed," I said, picking up my shirt next. "We need to buy you a horse and get you out of town."

***

I stood at the edge of Terrastera, watching Leif disappear down the road. We'd spend the morning procuring him a horse, supplies, clothing, weapons, and anything else he could need on the road. I showed him how to hide his money and gave him a few towns he might try. At last, with one final goodbye, he set off to the southeast, headed toward the coast. As I watched him go, I felt a sense of longing that I hadn't earned. It had been a long time since I'd spent that much time with someone without working a job.

It was sad, and I knew it. But that's how it was.

With a sigh, I straightened myself up, putting on my air of cocky confidence once more. I needed to find a job. There was enough coin in my pouch to get me through a couple of weeks of living in the city, but it wouldn't last forever. Thankfully Terrastera was rife with problems, and there were bounties posted everywhere. Not to mention the Clerics of the Twilight liked to hire people now and then to do their dirty work, which I wasn't above doing. All I needed to do was go to the local guard garrison. They always had a board posted with odd jobs.

An hour later, I found myself standing in front of that same board, a hand on my hip as I scanned through the postings. After a moment, I found what I was looking for, the highest-paying job. I tore the parchment off the board, unrolling it to peruse the details.

Wanted: Mercenaries to clear out the crystal mines

The Soroma Mines have been plagued by monsters from the deep. An expedition crew recently unearthed a natural cavern connecting to a vast series of natural tunnels below the city. Several miners have lost their lives, and the rest refuse to enter the mines until they are cleared. Creatures range from goblinoids to more enormous monsters such as spiders and other insects of unusual size. One animal, a crystal-eating worm, has caused the most damage.

A team of mercenaries, accompanied by a Cleric of the Twilight, will be sent in to clear the mines. All members that return with proof of death of the crystal-eating worm will be paid the total amount of this contract. Experience is required if you wish to retain your life—supplies are provided upon entrance to the mines.

Reward: 1000 gold pieces
Signed,
-Baron An'Cleth
Sky Serpent Shipping Co.

Well, a thousand gold pieces definitely caught my attention. Fighting monsters was my specialty, and being underground felt like home. All the Brotherhood hideouts were kept out of sight, usually deep under the cities where they'd been built. The job sounded perfect, with supplies provided and only a giant worm to kill. The only part I wasn't excited about was working with one of the Clerics.

The Clerics of the Twilight were the worst people in existence in all senses of the word. They were the pets of the state, the keepers of healing magic and religion in all of Eadronem. As such, they enjoyed a life of prosperity and ease, entirely provided by the state. Anyone who dared oppose them felt the full wrath of the government, the nobles, and the guards should they get involved. This, of course, led to the Clerics demanding whatever they wanted, and the people bowed to them without hesitation. The result was fat old men with healing powers ransoming their gifts to ordinary people, taking everything they had and giving them almost nothing in return. They were greedy and selfish, the worst kind of people I could imagine.

And now, if I wanted to make enough gold to set me up for years to come, I had to work with one.

"Just one time should be fine," I said under my breath, folding the paper and tucking it into my pocket. "Then I'm gone. Out of this city forever, I hope."

I tipped my head back, my eyes trailing up the mountain to the massive crystal floating between Terrastera and the floating city of Aratis, where all the nobles lived. Some Baron up there was losing his ass because of these creatures in the mines. I'm sure he had a fleet of airships sitting empty, waiting for their shipment of magically infused crystal that had yet to be dug out of the earth. Magic was rare these days and only increased the crystal's value. No wonder he was willing to pay a small fortune for it.

And I was about to take him for all he had.

Four: Dante

I stood at the ship's bow, the wind blowing in my face as the airship lifted away from the sky port. Orders were called out behind me, deckhands rushing back and forth to ensure the launch went off without a hitch. The thrum of magic hummed through the wooden boards under my feet, the crystal engines keeping it aloft. I closed my eyes, feeling the sudden surge of adrenaline through my body as the ship leaned forward and started to gain speed.

It took everything I had not to shout for joy as we sailed through the air, the top of the clouds approaching us fast. I felt my muscles tense as we struck the clouds, bracing myself for the sight about to open below me. I hadn't seen the lower world in seven years. Even on clear days, the haze made it hard to make out. But as we burst through the bottom of the clouds, I held my breath, leaning over the railing as far as I dared.

Fields and forests spread out below me, greenery stretching away in all directions. On the southern side of Terrastera, I could see the golden fields of wheat tended by farmers. Livestock kept to the eastern side while forests and rivers covered the north and the west. Level with the ship, I could see jagged rock, the underside of the floating island of Aratis. As we dipped further, the stones came to a point, like an upside-down mountain covered in vines and greenery clinging to the rock. The mountain of Terrastera rose up to meet it, the two peaks nearly touching. However, that wasn't what caught my attention.

There, hovering between the peaks of the mountains, was a massive amber crystal glowing as it slowly rotated in place. It was the Soroma Crystal, the source of all magic in Eadronem. Facets the size of whole neighborhoods caught the sunlight, reflecting it across the valley below in a spray of rainbow color. I'd seen drawings of it before, but never in person. It was more beautiful than I could have ever imagined. I stared open-mouthed, taking in every shine and shimmer from the crystal's surface. Even so far away from it, I could feel the waves of power rolling off it. It might have gone unnoticed to those not practiced in the arcane, but to me, it was like feeling warm ocean waves breaking over my body. It was incredible.

But just as soon as it came into view, the airship gathered more speed, angling around the mountain to head for the sky port below. I kept my eyes on the crystal for as long as possible until it slipped out of view behind the stone towers. The ship passed into the shadow of Aratis as we finally began to slow. I glanced over the edge, watching the gray city get closer and closer. I was surprised to see a complete lack of color; all the buildings were constructed from thatch, slate, and stone. The second thing I noticed was the smell as the wind shifted.

Calder hadn't been kidding. It really did smell like shit.

Doing my best to stomach the smell, I moved back toward the helm as we pulled lower in the sky. The captain called out orders, the deckhands continuing to rush about the deck. To my dismay, it looked like the trip would be a lot shorter than I expected. A small part of me wanted the ship to turn south and just fly out over the continent, headed toward whatever awaited us just past the horizon. But as the sounds of the sky port rose up from below us, that fantasy died away.

Taking a deep breath, I readied myself to depart. Behind me, I heard the captain's quarters open, the hinges squealing slightly. Turning, I watched as Master Ryker stepped out, another young acolyte behind him carrying a satchel and a stack of scrolls balanced in his arms. It looked like Ryker had more business to look to than just my mission while he was in the city. Hopefully, I could have everything done before he was ready to return. That might give me a leg up to get that promotion, goddess willing.

"The captain of the guard is awaiting your presence," Ryker said as I took my place next to him. "He'll brief you on the depth of the situation in the mines." He snapped at the acolyte behind him, who quickly produced a scroll from the pile held in his arms. Ryker took it and held it out toward me. "Give that to the captain with my regards."

"Yes, sir," I replied, taking the scroll.

"And another thing," he continued. "On my orders, the captain has made sure to hire a group of mercenaries that would... *not be missed* should something happen to them." He glanced down at me. "Your main objective is to get the job done, *not* ensure everyone makes it out safe."

I felt my shoulders tense as I realized what Ryker was saying. He noticed the change in my demeanor immediately.

"Acolyte Dante," he said, looking back over the ship's bow. "There are certain creatures in this world that walk among us, monstrous races that have a sordid history with mankind. You are aware of this, yes?"

"Y-Yes, sir..."

"It is the opinion of the Temple of the Twilight and the Goddess' will that these... *creatures* should eventually find their way out of Eadronem. Already their numbers have dwindled for the past few centuries. So much so, in fact, that we rarely see them in our cities. They don't have homes of their own, so they live on the fringes of our society, sucking our people dry in the process.' As it drew near, he gestured out over the railing at the city of Terrastera. "If there weren't so many monsters wandering around Terrastera, it would be a much nicer place. The people here lose their jobs to these creatures or are robbed in the streets. It's why the nobles have to keep themselves so separated. It's just not safe down here."

"I... I had no idea..."

Ryker nodded, placing his hand on my shoulder. "It's a terrible thing, but one that the Temple is slowly righting through the years. However, it only seems fit to hire monsters to kill other monsters," he added. "Better that we lose those that would do us harm instead of the good, hard-working people of Terrastera. Do you understand?"

"Yes, sir," I replied. "I understand completely."

"Good. Trust no one in the group. Some of them may look normal, masquerading as humans in the daylight, but they are undesirables through and through."

"Thank you for letting me know, sir."

I still couldn't help the cold feeling spreading through my chest at his words. There was something about it that didn't sit right with me. I'd never thought about it before, but everyone at the Temple was human. When I'd been an orphan living on the streets, several of my compatriots were Orcs or Draak. There was even one boy who had the power to change his shape, though I only saw him do it once when he tore a city guard to shreds. Needless to say, I never saw him again. Still, I didn't remember the others being bad at all. In fact, a few of them helped me now and then.

"An acolyte that would become a Cleric should be aware of the situation in the world."

My thoughts came to a screeching halt as I stared wide-eyed up at Ryker.

"A... A Cleric?"

"Should you complete your mission successfully," he nodded. "I see no reason why you wouldn't be promoted."

I felt my jaw muscles working momentarily, but no words fell from my lips. I'd hoped against hope that this mission would bring me closer to my goals, but I didn't believe it could actually happen. The Goddess of the Twilight had smiled down upon me at last, and I wouldn't waste her gifted opportunity. Pushing all doubts from my mind, I straightened myself and gave Ryker a curt nod.

"Yes, sir," I replied. "Thank you, sir."

Ryker nodded in return as the ship's captain shouted more orders to the deckhands. A moment later, I felt the ship shudder under my feet as we touched down in the sky port, the crystalline engine's whine slowly dying away as it came to rest. The sails were drawn up, ropes tied off, and a gangplank was put in place.

"You have your orders Acolyte Dante," Ryker said, heading for the exit. "We return to the Temple in four days. Be sure that you're finished and returned by then."

"Yes, sir."

With a flurry of white robes, Ryker exited the ship, the young acolyte behind him jogging to keep up. However, I stood on the ship's deck for a long moment, letting his words sink in as the crew rushed around me. I was going to be a Cleric, a full Temple of the Twilight member at last! Calder would lose his damn mind when I told him! Being a Cleric provided so many privileges that I'd been dreaming about for years. In fact, I might even be able to request an acolyte of my own and take Calder on my adventures. He'd been wanting out of the Temple for a long time, and at last, I could repay him for all his friendship throughout the years.

A new life was starting, and I wouldn't let anything get in my way. The Goddess taught us to put aside emotions for the world's greater good, and I would do just that. If she and Master Ryker thought these... *creatures* were harming the world, then I would make it my duty to see that they didn't return from the mission. After all, the will of the Goddess had taken me this far; the least I could do was show her a bit of faith in return.

With the scroll clutched in my hand, I crossed the gangplank out into the city with my head held high. I was a Cleric of the Twilight, and there was nothing I couldn't accomplish.

Five: Ronan

Guards stood around the entrance to the mine, their dark leather armor engraved with the symbol of the state. It was the likeness of the Soroma Crystal, the one that hovered between Terrastera and Aratis. Everyone knew they were dogs to the nobles, so I did my best to steer clear of them. But not this morning.

According to the garrison office, I'd taken the job to help clear the mines along with a handful of other mercenaries. For the past two days, I'd spent all my time eating and drinking at one of the local taverns, doing my best to ignore the almost permanent darkness that fell over Terrastera every day.

There was a sudden splash as the water struck the street behind me as if someone had emptied a bucket out a window. But there were no buildings around me, just a giant open courtyard that served as the entrance to the mine. I glanced upward at the floating city nearly a mile above my head. Aratis not only enjoyed fair weather and sun every day of the year, but they also didn't have to worry about their garbage or sewers. Piping ran through the rock, directing any liquid, from house or street, out to the bottom of the city, where it fell on the unsuspecting citizens of Terrastera. The people were used to it, but it took almost every fiber of my being to ignore the sewage smell that permeated the entire city. Just another reason to hate the nobles literally pissing on their constituents and employees.

"You here for the mine job?" a gruff voice said behind me.

I spun around to see a tall man with green skin and tusks sticking out from his bottom jaw. He was clad in rough-looking leather armor and stained clothes. The black hair on his head had been braided back into a single short chain reaching his shoulders.

Orcs were not a common sight in places like Terrastera. They tended to keep to the north in the mountains where they couldn't be found. Too many times, the state had labeled them as feral and dangerous, especially when it benefited them to start a hostile land takeover. I was surprised to see one working for the very people that hated his kind.

"Yeah," I replied, keeping my thoughts to myself. "Pays good."

"Pays *damn good*," the orc nodded with a smile. "Else, I wouldn't be here."

"You and me both."

"Name's Kai," he said, holding out a large green hand.

I shook it. "Ronan."

"Good to see we've got some muscle on this trip," he added, giving me a wink. "Wouldn't want the *wolves* to get us in our sleep, huh?"

He was being coy, but what he meant was all too obvious. Orcs had great senses, much like the werewolves in my clan. He could smell my true nature, and it put me on edge. But I wasn't one to show it. Instead, I squared my shoulders and lifted my chin.

"Wolves are the least of our worries there," I replied.

"I ain't worried about em," he said, giving me a small smirk. "Plenty of wolves back home I've known all my life. They're good people if they can tame the beast."

"Taming a beast makes it weak. It's knowing when to let it *out* that's most important. Funneling those animalistic urges can be... *beneficial*."

"I like the way you think, brother," he replied, clapping me on the back.

"You there!"

Both Kai and I turned around, glancing up at a chubby man dressed in ill-fitting plate armor. His straps had been stretched to the limits by his rotund form, but the armor and the crest on his shoulder identified him as a high-ranking guard officer. Typical that he should insist on wearing armor he clearly hadn't used in years. Plate was never that clean unless it was meticulously scrubbed and polished every single day. Fighters, *real ones*, didn't have time for that kind of bullshit.

"If you aren't here for the job, shove off!" he called, giving us a simple wave of his hand.

I started off toward him with Kai close behind me. As I approached, the man squared himself up, trying to look intimidating. But as I came to a stop in front of him, the color went from his face. I towered a full head and shoulders above him, my chest wider than his entire body. Resting my hand on the hilt of my great sword, I looked down at him.

"We're here for the job," I growled, baring my teeth at him. "Who the hell are you?"

The man immediately looked affronted, puffing out his chest at me. "I'll have you know I'm the captain of the guard for the entire city!" He placed his hands on his hips, furrowing his brow. "I'm *very* important."

"Of course you are," I nodded, not doing a thing to hide my sarcasm. "So, Captain of the Guard, are you going to show us where we need to go for this job you have to hire outside help for?"

I heard Kai behind me snicker, but the captain looked less than entertained by my snide remarks. He cleared his throat, pulling open a roll of parchment in front of him. The back of it bore the seal of the state in blood-red ink.

"Names?" he demanded.

"Kai Hammerfist," the orc next to me said.

The captain scanned for a minute. "Right. You can go through." He turned his glare on me. "And you, smart ass?"

"Ronan Fangborn," I replied, not backing down from him.

He looked over the parchment, his brows knitting together as he came to rest on a name. With a sigh, he rolled it up, tucking it back into the satchel at his side.

"Follow me," he said, clearly annoyed that we were supposed to be there. "We'll brief you in the garrison."

He headed toward the far end of the square, where a low building had harsh square windows enveloped by bars. Kai and I followed close behind, giving each other a knowing glance.

A few minutes later, we found ourselves huddled up inside a meeting chamber in the back of the garrison. Guards were stationed at the doors as if they thought we were about to cause trouble. That was their way, though, and not at all surprising. Those who joined the guard were quickly brainwashed to worship the state and the nobles that ran it. They dedicated their entire lives, even after retirement, to defending the state at all costs. Normal people went in, and when they came out, they were hardly recognizable, so full of hate and false pride that they could barely function. I hated working with them, but they always paid the most. If I wanted to eat, that's what I had to put up with.

There were a few others in the room as well, a rag-tag group of nobodies that looked like they were in the same line of work as me. Two dark-skinned humans, a male, and a female, kept close to one another, whispering in a language I didn't understand. Both were dressed in dark blue tunics, their leather armor stained black. Tucked away in the corner was a Draak, one of the more rare people in all of Eadronem. He would have looked mostly human if not for his dark curling horns, the splotches of black scales speckled across his body, and his long curling tail. He wore a simple brown robe that covered most of his skin. All I could see was his head and the scaled hands ending in claws. In his right hand was a staff made of twisted wood.

It was uncommon to see a mage unmolested by the Clerics of the Twilight. However, given his lineage, he'd probably been ignored on purpose. Almost all Clerics were human, specializing in healing magic. However, Draak were known to be gifted in elemental magic, especially that of fire and acid, but never in healing. I glanced in his direction and gave him a small nod as our eyes met. He returned the gesture. I had no doubt he already knew I was a werewolf, but that put us on the same side. It was always us against the humans, and if we wanted to survive, we had to have each other's backs.

"Everyone's here, so let's get this over with," the captain said, stepping to the front of the room. "The goal is simpl–"

He stopped as the door to the room opened once more. I glanced back as a hooded figure clad in white stepped into the meeting chamber. The figure reached up, pulling his hood back to reveal a young man, probably in his mid-twenties, with blonde hair, blue eyes, and pale skin that looked as if it had never been touched by sunlight. He looked almost angelic with the golden circlet placed upon his head. In the center of it was set a small stone, a piece of the Soroma Crystal. That, along with the golden setting sun embroidered into his robes, marked him as a Cleric of the Twilight.

I hated him the moment I saw him.

His robes were too clean, his skin too flawless, and his eyes too crystalline. Everything about him was perfect and pristine, the exact opposite of myself and everyone else in Eadronem. Only rich people could get to such a state of cleanliness while the rest of us walked through streets as filth rained down upon us. I had no doubt in my mind that he was just as greedy as the rest of his order, stepping on as many people as possible to get what he wanted.

But I also couldn't help the stirrings in my nether regions as I eyed him up and down. Even with the robe, I could make out his lithe and delicate figure. His face was all angles while retaining a softness that made me wonder what it would be like to press his lips against mine. I wanted to rip that white robe off of him and pin him down in the dirt, showing him how good it felt to get down and dirty once in a while. In my mind's eye, I could see him lying in front of me, my cock buried in his ass as he begged for more. Just think of it, one of the high and mighty begging for a good fuck from nothing but a dirty werewolf, the shunned of society.

I shook my head, attempting to get rid of the sudden onslaught of thoughts racing through my mind. The cleric and I were mortal enemies. Nothing was ever going to happen between us. However, I pinned the thoughts aside, promising myself I'd revisit them when I had some alone time.

"Continue, Captain," the man said, his tenor voice clear and commanding.

He moved with poise and purpose and an air of confidence that was most definitely annoying. As he made his way to the front, the captain cleared his throat, drumming his armored fingers on the table nervously.

"Right. As I was saying, the goal of this expedition is simple. Get in, kill the worm, get out." He held up a finger to punctuate his next remark. "*With proof.* There will be no payment if there's no proof. The Baron needs to be sure that this has been handled once and for all."

The cleric stepped up beside him, turning to face the room with his hands laced in front of him. His eyes flicked to each person in the room, but when he got to me, they stopped. For a long moment, we stared at one another, silence filling the space around us. I got irritated with his stares and bared my teeth at him, a low growl rumbling in my throat. His brows furrowed as he turned away, lifting his nose into the air.

"The Baron has been most gracious to enlist the services of a Cleric of the Twilight," the captain said, gesturing to the man beside him. "He will lend his powers to keep you safe and healed on your journey should you encounter unexpected dangers."

"I am Acolyte Dante," the cleric said, his voice ringing through the room. "I will protect you to the best of my ability as I lead you through the mines. I have been briefed on the location of our target and what dangers we'll meet along the way. Follow my leadership, and together we will be victorious in this endeavor."

A mouthful of pretty words, as usual. I scoffed, and Dante's eyes flashed in my direction once more. He was just an acolyte, a nobody within his own order, and yet he strutted around like he was the general of the whole fucking army. Talk about being too big for your britches.

"We leave in one hour," Dante said, pulling his eyes away from me. "Gather your supplies and regroup at the entrance to the mines. If all goes well, we'll be back in less than two days."

He headed purposefully toward the exit, nodding to each of us as he went. But when he got to me, he gave me a once-over and lifted his nose into the air.

"And clean yourself up," he added, nodding in my direction. "Just because you're a sellsword dog doesn't mean you have to smell like one."

I growled as he walked by, losing control of my emotions. I wasn't sure if I wanted to slit his throat or fuck him, the latter of which I found highly irritating. Who did this little privileged fuck think he was? This was why I hated the Clerics. They were always so haughty and full of themselves, thinking they did nothing wrong while they stepped all over the hard-working people of the world.

One thing was for sure; I was going to finish this job and get paid. But, along the way, I was going to teach this asshole a lesson. It was time the Clerics were brought down a notch. And maybe it would take a *dog* to do it.

Six: Ronan

An hour later, with a heavy pack strapped to my shoulders, I stood at the entrance to the crystal mines with Kai at my side. We'd hit it off and had agreed to have each other's back on the job. Making friends as a mercenary wasn't a thing, but having a comrade, you could count on while in the depths of a mine or in the middle of a battle was something that all of us did. Our lives might be full of solitude, but we watched out for one another. And, with a job like this one, there was no sense of competition. We'd all get paid the same amount if we made it out alive. 'A rising tide lifts all boats' sort of thing.

Soon after we'd arrived, a pair of humans showed up, each of them with a smaller pack. I couldn't tell if they were partners or siblings, but between the wicked blade the woman held and the quiver of dark arrows the man had, they looked to be plenty capable. I gave them a friendly nod, and they returned the gesture before returning to chatter in their own language. I had a feeling we wouldn't be able to communicate verbally, but that didn't matter. All I needed was for them to defend the group when the time came.

The last to arrive, with no visible pack, was the Draak mage in his dark brown robes. All he held was the staff in his right hand and a small satchel draped across his body. The trip was only going to take us a couple of days, but still, I couldn't imagine going without food for all that time. Then again, I wasn't familiar with Draak and their ways, so maybe he was fine. Either way, I gave him a small nod as he arrived. He looked me up and down before returning it and walked over to the stone wall, where he took a seat. Reaching into his bag, he pulled out a small book and began to read.

"So, this is gonna be a piece of cake, don't you think?" Kai said, putting his pack down on the ground. He already had a heavy hammer strapped to his back, and his pack was bigger than anyone else's. "Ain't ever seen so many people worked up by a worm before."

"It's not just a worm," the Draak replied from a few feet away, not looking up from his book.

"A worm is a worm," Kai said with a grin. "Doesn't matter how big they are; they all take a punch just like anything else."

The Draak sighed, shaking his head. "Whatever you say," he said sarcastically. "You know best."

Kai's brows furrowed, and I put a hand on his shoulder to stop him from moving toward the man. The last thing we needed was a fight before we even got started.

"What do you know?" I asked, giving Kai a look that told him to calm down. "Any information is helpful if we want to get through this as easily as possible. Those guards knew jack-shit."

The Draak looked up at me. "A wolf with horse sense, that's a rarity."

I smirked. "I'm not just a pretty face, you know."

"Ah, there it is," he sighed again, flipping the book closed. Pushing himself back to his feet, he tucked the book away and stepped over to us. "The crystal-eating worm is a bit more problematic than they're making it out to be."

The human pair nearby perked up, taking a step closer.

"In what way?"

"For one, its body processes the crystal and turns it into armor, so it will be very hard to damage. It will most likely be anywhere between twenty and thirty feet long, its mouth large enough to swallow us whole."

Kai grimaced.

"Exactly," the Draak nodded. "Not to mention, the crystal it eats is inherently magical. It will not only be resistant to magic, but it may have powers of its own." He glanced at each one of us in turn. "There's a reason the reward is so high for this job... and why the last two groups that went in didn't come back out."

"That's why they hired a cleric," I muttered. "The Baron must be desperate to pay such a price."

"True. And should a cleric fall in the mines, it would incite a response from their order, bringing the full might of the Twilight down on the monster within." He glanced around before leaning in close. "We are most likely not meant to succeed in this endeavor."

"Well, too fuckin' bad for them," Kai laughed. "Ain't no way I'm dyin' in some hole in the ground because of a worm."

The Draak smiled. "My sentiments exactly."

"Glad to see we're of the same mind," I nodded, holding out a hand. "The name's Ronan."

"Torval," the Draak replied, shaking my hand.

"We follow," the human man next to me added. "You lead."

His speech was stilted, but he must have picked up enough to understand what was going on. It was good to know we were all on the same page. I gave him a small smile, opening my mouth to reply just as a voice rose up behind us.

"Mercenaries!"

It was the fat man again in his too-small armor. Beside him stood the cleric Dante. He'd traded his stark white cloak for a black one that looked more functional. On his left side was a small leather bag, the straps cinched around his waist and leg to hold it in place. A bandolier crossed his chest, and several vials of glowing red liquid buttoned in place. I'd seen a couple of healing potions in my lifetime, but never this many in one place. In his right hand was a four-foot-long crystalline wand that came to a sharp point on either end. It looked almost clear in the sunlight, the facets catching the light and throwing rainbows all over the ground. It seemed extremely fragile, but I'd heard too many stories about the cleric's power to write it off. Magic was not something to be underestimated, especially when it came from their order.

But, beyond all of that, I noticed how handsome Dante was. His new clothing showed off his lean body, accentuating every curve and muscle. He might not have been built like Kai and me, but he was a fine specimen nonetheless. I found myself wondering what he'd feel like wrapped up in my arms and what he'd taste like as I licked every square inch of his body. What noises would he make when I took him in my mouth, a finger or two massaging him from the inside? I bet they were delicious.

"And with that, be on your way!" the captain called.

I'd missed his entire speech, too caught up in my fantasies about Dante to hear a thing. As my thoughts returned to normal, I realized I was staring up at the cleric, and his blue eyes were glaring back at me. In a flash, the fantasy fell away, and I remembered how much I despised him and everything he stood for.

He pulled his gaze away from me, turning up his nose once more. "Time to go," he said, adjusting the grip on his wand and heading toward the opening to the mine. "I'd like to be done with this as soon as possible."

"Missing your cushy life already, cleric?" I said as he passed.

He stopped, turning to face me. "No," he replied, staring up at me. "I'm just already tired of the stench rolling off you."

I crossed my arms over my chest, taking a step forward so that I was towering over him. "You think you're tough, don't you, pretty boy?"

Dante did not back down. In fact, he met my posturing head-on, challenging me in a way that I wasn't used to. Usually, people just backed down, but this guy had guts. However, he had no idea he was standing up to a werewolf. If I wanted to, I could shift into my monstrous form and tear him limb from limb. Then again, maybe he'd be into that. There was more than one person out there that wanted to be fucked by a werewolf.

"I don't need to be tough," he sneered. "Turns out, when you're not a big fucking idiot, life gets a lot easier."

"Why you little basta—"

"Lead the way," Torval interjected, placing himself between me and Dante. He locked his gaze on me. "We're here to follow your orders and get the job done. Isn't that right, Ronan?"

I huffed, pulling myself away from him. "Sure. Whatever."

"Good to see there's *some* intelligent people on this expedition," Dante scoffed, turning away from us both. "Move out, everyone! We've got ground to cover, and I don't want to waste any unnecessary time."

I wanted to go after him, to *prove* to him I wasn't stupid, even if it meant using my fists. But Torval held me back, his strength surprising me.

"Leave it be," he muttered. "We don't want any trouble."

"Little runt isn't worth it," Kai said on my other side. "Tanglin' with a cleric is a one-way ticket to a jail cell."

"I know," I retorted, pulling myself away from Torval. "But he's just so... *infuriating*."

"You're the one throwing insults at him first," Torval replied, lifting an eyebrow. "None of us like the clerics, but that's no reason to go starting trouble. If you hate him that much, just keep your mouth shut and stay away from him."

"Just think of the gold," Kai added. "A whole chest of it to yourself. You can go wherever you want after this job. You could even get out of mercenary work for good."

"Yeah," I grumbled, letting my hands drop to my sides. "You're right."

A thousand gold was no small amount. Even with my bleeding heart, I would still have enough left over to do whatever I wanted for some time. My future could be whatever I needed it to be. I could even try to find Leif again on the coast, or at least someone like him. Mercenary work was fun and exciting, but I'd never told anyone what I really longed for. If I found the right man, one that *looked* like Dante that didn't come with a bunch of political bullshit, I might be tempted to hang up my sword for good.

I glanced up at the cleric as he stepped up to the mouth of the mines. He turned back, waiting for the rest of us to catch up. With a few whispered words and a swish of his wand, a ball of light appeared above his head, floating in the air. The light made him look even more angelic, giving him a warm glow that made me want to scoop him up in my arms and worship his body with my own.

"You dumbasses coming or what?" he called.

And, just like that, the feeling was gone.

What a fucking dickhead. I made a mental note to change my preferences for men. I wanted one that looked *nothing* like Dante because I had a feeling I'd be spending the rest of my life despising him.

With a low growl, I adjusted my pack and headed for the mine with the others. This was going to be a *long* job.

Seven: Dante

I really had my work cut out for me. The last thing I expected as the cleric of the group was to be leading the charge into the mines. However, when no one seemed to step forward and offer to lead, I took it upon myself. At the entrance, it didn't seem like such a big deal, but the further we delved, the more uncomfortable I became.

For the past seven years of my life, I'd lived in a multi-story temple on a massive rock floating in the sky. The passing clouds far below did nothing to turn my stomach, and I found the airship ride more thrilling than anything else. But being underground was something completely alien to me, and I didn't like it. It was as if the entire weight of the world was above my head, the rocks threatening to crush me should I speak too loudly or let my steps echo too far. Nothing stopped the earth from crashing down on me except for a few splintered beams of wood that looked as if they'd seen *much* better days.

I was having a hard time breathing, and my thoughts were racing.

A strange weight on my shoulder made me gasp in surprise, spinning around with the torch wielded like a sword in front of me.

"Are you all right?" a deep voice asked, vibrating from the dark figure in front of me.

The torch shifted to the left as a hand pressed against my forearm. With the light off to the side, my eyes could adjust, and I saw the tall Draak man standing in front of me. He was thick from head to toe, his neck nearly as big around as my head. Even so, I knew he was small for his kind. His dark cloak shifted as he leaned against his staff, his dark eyes staring down at me.

"I... I'm fine," I replied, at last, cutting through the awkward silence.

"Is this your first time underground?"

What the hell? Could Draak read people's minds or something? How did he know exactly what was bothering me? Even if he'd guessed right, I was still leery to admit it. I wasn't sure if the information could be used against me at some point. Master Ryker had been clear to not trust these beasts, and I didn't want to disobey him. Still, I couldn't think of a fast enough excuse.

"Y-Yes," I said shakily, trying to gather my thoughts. "I've lived in Aratis for several years. I'm afraid I'm not used to this kind of... terrain."

"Many people fear the dark underground where the light cannot penetrate, and the very rocks themselves seem to threaten to snuff you out in an instant."

Yep. That about summed it up.

"But don't worry," he added, giving me a small toothy smile. "This mine is stable."

"How do you know?"

"I can feel it." He closed his eyes, placing a hand against the damp stone wall. "There is no tremor, no vibration in the stones. They are at peace." His dark orbs flashed in the torchlight as he opened his eyes once again. "The miners were careful to cut a stable path. Their families have been delving for generations. You have nothing to fear."

I furrowed my brows, not quite sure if I believed him or not. "Th-Thank you..."

"You gonna sit around and chat all day or get the fuck out of the way?"

I glanced up at the gruff man staring down at me, his dark brown eyes full of malice. It took everything I had to hold back the snide remark that I wanted to make to him. Instead, I merely stepped to the side, gesturing for him to lead. He snorted, giving me a dirty look before taking the torch from my hands and heading further in. The Draak beside me merely shook his head and followed after.

I fell in step behind them, the orc and the other human-looking pair behind me. The torch bobbed ahead of us, the rude man leading the way. I'd never met anyone with such a bad attitude in my life. He looked human enough, but that couldn't be right. Master Ryker had said everyone on the mission was a monster, except me, of course. He was big enough, I supposed, his arms bulging and a wide, muscular chest trapped under his leather armor. Not to mention he was nearly as tall as the orc. That couldn't be natural.

But that didn't stop me from staring as we continued through the mine. His ass was outlined perfectly in those dark leather pants, the seams straining under his girth. I'd only caught a glimpse of the front a couple of times, and that leather looked like it was under *a lot* more stress. The guy was nothing but muscles and raw sex appeal. I was almost ashamed to admit how happy I was to be behind him, where I could stare without worry of being caught. I'd grown up in a temple full of men, and since attachments were forbidden, so were romantic relationships. However, that didn't stop everyone in the temple from fucking each other all the time.

And yet, somehow, that didn't feel like what I was experiencing with this guy. Sure, he was incredibly attractive, but there was something else, an almost animalistic urge to drag him off into the nearest alcove and let him have his way with me. But I couldn't understand why. The guy was a raging dickhead. The last thing I wanted was for him to be within fifty feet of me, much less with his dick rammed up my ass. However, I couldn't deny that the images flashing through my head didn't turn me on, especially when my pants grew much tighter than usual. I was glad to have the cloak as I pulled it closer around me. Being turned on was one thing, but I didn't know what these other creatures might do if they noticed my arousal.

"Feeling better?"

I nearly jumped out of my skin, not realizing that the Draak had fallen in step beside me. I'd been so caught up in my rugged mercenary fantasy that I didn't even notice him.

"W-What?" I stammered, pulling the cloak tighter. "Y-Yeah. Much better now. Thanks."

"Good. I'm glad to hear it," he nodded. "My name is Torval, by the way."

"Dante."

"It is nice to meet you, Dante. It's not often a Draak like myself gets a chance to speak with a cleric on such a personal level."

"I've never spoken to a Draak before," I replied, taking a deep breath to clear the smutty images from my mind. It was difficult enough to walk on wet stones without having to worry about my dick. "Or, well, I knew a couple when I was a child, but that was before I was taken in by the Temple."

"You are very lucky," he said, nodding his head once more. "To show magical potential in the healing arts is a rare gift and one that comes with great benefits."

"Benefits?"

The Draak arched his eyebrow. "Yes, of course."

"I'm not sure I understand."

"Let me put it this way," he said. "You do not have to worry about finding work, making gold, or where your next meal will come from for the rest of your life. It's true that clerics travel and do work, but there is always a need for healing." His hand tightened around his staff, lifting it a few inches into the air. "But for people like me... well, destructive elemental magic is feared by most. I'm afraid both my race and my power put most of Eadronem's people ill at ease."

"Is that why you became a mercenary?"

He nodded, placing his staff back on the ground. "Yes. That... and I was driven from my home at a young age."

"Why?"

"Learning to control power such as mine is dangerous... especially without a teacher."

"The acolytes at the temple can be dangerous too sometimes when they're young," I replied, trying to keep the conversation going. "While it's true that the temple takes care of and trains us, there are some things that can't be taught. A handful of students die every year from overextending their power."

"Oh?"

"The Goddess of the Twilight teaches us that healing magic comes from the very lifeforce of the wielder. While it's possible to do great things, that power needs to be trained, like a muscle, until it can handle normal everyday problems like broken bones or deep cuts. Should a student attempt to mend a broken arm before they are trained, the effort sucks the very life out of them, leaving them nothing but a mummified shell."

The Draak's eyes went wide. "That... That is terrible."

I nodded. "It is horrible to witness. But I'm sure your power is similar."

He slowly shook his head. "No. My power doesn't come from my being but from nature around me." He gestured out to the wet stones flashing in the torchlight. "There is only so much I can channel through my body each day, which tires me out, but not to the point of death." He paused for a moment. "However, there are times when the power flows unchecked like the weave of magic opens wide and allows anything through."

I'd never heard of such a thing before. But the thought of free-flowing magic caused a prickle of fear to crawl up the back of my neck. I'd seen acolytes consumed by their spells, but mages that could access unlimited power could destroy all of Eadronem in a flash if they wanted. No human could do that, and I was starting to understand why Master Ryker didn't trust the Draak or his companions. Even a well-intentioned person couldn't be trusted with that amount of magic. It would corrupt anyone.

"That's why I had to leave my home," he added sadly, his eyes cast downward. "But it hasn't happened again. I've learned to control and focus myself for my and others' safety. Do not worry."

"I'll... try not to..."

With that, the Draak sped up once more, placing himself between me and the asshole with the torch. I stared for a few minutes, my thoughts racing about what he'd told me. There were so many questions I had, things that the Temple had forbidden us to know about other kinds of magic. What the Draak wielded was technically illegal, not that it stopped people like him from being hired for missions just like the one we were on. Mages were rare, most of them never reaching adulthood, and now I understood why. Their power was dangerous, to say the very least.

And yet, even with all that on my mind, I couldn't help shifting my eyes up toward the muscular man once more. The squeak of his leather, the curves of his ass, and the sweat beading on his arms drove the Draak completely from my mind. Within a few seconds, I was rock hard again, staring at the man that I was fairly certain I hated more than anyone else in the world. But I couldn't shake the images from my head, the fantasy playing itself out over and over.

Suddenly he stopped, the torchlight illuminating a stone intersection ahead. There was a path to the left and one that went straight on. The other's glanced around at one another, but my gaze was fixed on him, still drinking in every inch of his beautiful form.

"Which way?" he said, his gaze coming to rest on me.

"Huh?" I was too busy staring at his bulge to think of much else. "What?"

"Which *fucking* way, dumbass?" he replied, pointing at the tunnel.

Well, that broke the spell.

Burning him the dirtiest look I could muster, I unlatched my bag and pulled out a small map. To my dismay, I had to get closer to him and the torch so I could see. The moment I was near, I felt him step up beside me, his body so close that I could feel the waves of heat rolling off him in the cold underground. The scent of warm leather and sweat washed over me, but there was something else there, a spiciness like cinnamon or other rare herbs found only in the far south. I breathed it in deeply, savoring the smell.

"Well?" he insisted, looming over me.

"To... To the left," I replied at last, tracing my finger over the page. "That's where the miners broke into the natural caverns below."

"Fucking finally," he huffed.

With that, he turned on his heel, stomping down the tunnel once more. His scent left with him, and my head cleared, the irritation taking its place.

I didn't care how good he smelled or looked. The plain truth was that he was a dick. And I really didn't like him.

Eight: Ronan

"Break!" Dante called from the front, holding up a hand to stop us. "Take ten minutes to catch your breath." He pointed a finger in my direction. "Hey, stinky! Scout ahead and make sure there's no monsters in front of us."

I felt my fists ball up at my sides. If he didn't stop calling me names, I was going to bury him in the nearest ravine. It wouldn't take much to put him down, not with those skinny fucking arms. Clerics were notorious for being rather breakable if you could get close enough. We'd have to sleep at some point. If the job wasn't offering such a large amount of money, I might have given in to the urge. Plus... it seemed like a waste to cut up such a pretty face.

By the gods... what was wrong with me? This guy was an asshole, and I despised him. I needed to stop letting my mind wander.

"Hey!" Dante called again, snapping his fingers. "You deaf now? Get moving!"

Those feelings left immediately, and I felt the rage seep back into my limbs.

"I'll go with ya," Kai offered.

But I waved him off. "I'm fine." I glared back at Dante. "Wouldn't want to undermine the pretty boy's authority. I'm sure this is the first time he's been allowed out of the temples on his own."

He returned the glare, opening his mouth to retort, but I ignored him as I stomped off down the tunnel. I was around the corner and out of sight before he could get the words out.

"Good," I muttered under my breath. "Little bastard is too big for his britches to begin with."

Scouting was probably my least favorite part of being on jobs like this one. Usually, we would go in pairs to raise our chances of survival should something come up, but I was feeling too proud to accept help. Grasping a torch in my left hand, I moved down the tunnel, trying to be as quiet as possible. I already knew there were monsters lurking in the dark, and I mentally chastised myself for going alone. It had been a stupid decision to refuse Kai's help. Hopefully, it didn't cost me my life.

However, as I stopped some three hundred feet off from the rest of the group to listen, I heard nothing. The tunnels seemed to be deserted. I lifted my nose to the air, trying to pick up any unfamiliar scents. All I could make out was damp stone, metallic minerals, and a faint bit of the clean, perfumed smell that always seemed to hang around Dante. I caught myself breathing it in hungrily, trying to get more of it. There was something about his scent that was so appealing, and I couldn't resist it. I made a quick mental note to never get too close to him, which should be easy, considering how much I wanted to deck him in the face every fucking second of the day.

Shaking my head, I walked over to the side of the cavern to relieve myself. I'd just finished when I heard something echo down through the tunnel. My ears perked up, my wolven senses on high alert. It happened again... then again. There was a strange clicking sound so soft it would have been inaudible to anyone else except a wolf. At first, I thought it might be bugs, but the longer I listened, the more it sounded like nails clicking on stone.

The twang of a bowstring was the only thing that warned me of the incoming arrow. Without seeing it, I dodged to the side, rolling across the stone floor and back to my feet. In an instant, I had my sword drawn, the steel flashing in the torchlight. Just beyond the edge of the light, I heard a frustrated grunt and the clatter of wooden arrows as another was drawn. Lifting the torch higher, I caught the faint outline of over a dozen dark, squat shapes moving in the distance. A flash of green eyes glared back at me, only three feet off the ground. Chittering quickly followed as another arrow was fired my way. Ducking and rolling again, I sprinted back toward the group, knowing I was outnumbered.

There were goblins in the tunnels, and there was only one thing they were after.

Fresh meat.

"GOBLINS!" I howled down the tunnel, my voice echoing off the stone. "ARM YOURSELVES!"

The chittering cackles behind me rose into a cacophony of war cries. Claws struck against stone as more than a dozen pairs of feet began to race in my direction. They were small but fast. My ears caught the twang of bowstrings as they ran, and I weaved back and forth, trying to avoid as many arrows as I could. They clattered off the stone around me, some skipping and bouncing off my armor. Goblins weren't the most formidable foes, but they were ruthless and determined. Their strength lay in numbers, overwhelming their targets in an ambush. My heart raced as I ran, the torch flickering in my grasp.

It wasn't every day the wolf became the prey, and I wasn't a fan.

I could make out the torches up ahead, their flames illuminating the chamber where the group had stopped to rest. Silhouetted against the flames was Kai, holding his warhammer aloft. He cried out as he saw me, his rage-filled voice reverberating off the walls. I heard a couple of the goblins hiss back, but they didn't slow.

Sliding to a stop next to Kai, I turned to face my pursuers, my chest heaving from the sudden sprint.

"Over... a dozen," I gasped. "Several archers. Not sure... what else."

"Don't make no difference to me," Kai growled. "They smash just the same."

"Funnel them through the gap!" I heard Dante call behind us. "We'll stop the wave before it crashes over us!"

Arrows bounced off the stone around us as Kai, and I glanced at one another. I could see in his eyes he wanted to rush in, to use his hammer to mow down the disgusting creatures. A part of me wanted to do the same, but I knew there were too many to come out unscathed.

If we funneled them through the tunnel, we might stand a chance of taking minimal damage.

"Come on," I cried, grabbing Kai by the shoulder. "Behind the wall!"

Kai grunted in irritation but followed me nonetheless. More arrows struck the stone around us as we took cover on opposite sides of the tunnel entrance. I could still hear the goblins rushing forward, their pace undaunted by our display. Glancing about the room, I saw the human woman with an arrow nocked, ducking behind a large stalagmite. Her companion had his sword drawn, rushing toward us to help guard the entrance. In the back of the cave were Torval and Dante, the staff and wand at the ready. I could already see the flames flickering at the end of Torval's staff as the elemental magic began to gather.

Those goblins wouldn't know what hit them.

I peeked around the edge of the tunnel to see a horde of goblins, probably close to thirty of them, rushing in our direction. Their flesh was gray-green and pale, their skin having never seen the light of day. Large black orb-like eyes stared back, glowing green where they caught the reflection of the firelight. They had floppy pointed ears that stuck straight out from the sides of their face and a maw full of shark-like teeth. Every inch of them was knobby, fat, and warted except for their strangely thin limbs. I watched as several of them held up their rusted swords or handmade clubs, prepared to attack us the moment they broke through the entrance.

But I wasn't going to let them make it that far.

However, I didn't get a chance to swing my sword before a beam of red light shot between Kai and me, striking the stone floor in front of the goblin ambush. We only had a fraction of a second to pull ourselves behind the stone before an earth-shattering boom echoed down the tunnel, followed by a ball of fire. Flames rushed into the space, consuming all the air around us and making it hard to breathe for a moment. Smoke and ash swirled up through the air, and I lifted my cloak to cover my mouth. A second later, the stench of burning hair and meat struck my nostrils, making my eyes water. I glanced up at Torval, his staff outstretched, bereft of sparking flames.

He was a lot more powerful than I thought.

But I didn't have time to think about it as more goblins, some partially burned, rushed into the cave despite their charred brethren. Both Kai and I cried out at the same time as we rushed the group. Several goblin bodies went sailing through the air with a bone-cracking blow from Kai's hammer. I swung my sword down, cleaving a singed goblin in two before following through to strike another nearby. The human man joined the fray at the same moment, his steel flashing as he let loose a series of quick cuts. In a matter of seconds, several goblins fell to the ground dead. But there were still more streaming in.

Arrows rained down on us as several archers in the back of the group took aim. Some fell on their companions, while others only struck the stone. However, a handful of them found their mark. I watched as Kai took three to the chest, the small arrows looking almost comical compared to his large form. He easily swept them away, breaking the shafts and lifting his hammer to rain down pain on more of the pitiful creatures. The human man had one sticking out of his left leg, but he ignored it as he continued to slash.

I hissed through my teeth as one found my shoulder, piercing a little deeper than I anticipated. However, that wasn't what bothered me. The moment it plunged into the muscle, I felt a burning sensation followed by a pulse through my system. I knew it was poisoned before the fungal scent hit my nostrils. Werewolves were strong against such things but not immune, and I knew I had only a minute or so to do away with this enemy before it started to slow my movements. I probably wouldn't die, but I'd be sluggish for a bit, and that didn't bode well when we were being overrun by vermin.

Cutting down another goblin, I heard something over the din. My wolf senses were on high alert, picking up the sound easily. There was a pounding of feet some distance off, coming down the tunnel toward us. While we'd already dispatched at least half of the initial force, I heard at least twenty more headed our way. The boom of the fire spell must have drawn them out.

Another volley of arrows came down on top of us, but we couldn't dodge out of the way as we were hemmed in by goblins on all sides. Several arrows struck Kai, a couple more into the human man, and a handful flew over our heads toward the other members of the group. I felt another sink into my arm and one into my thigh. There was another burst of poison in my bloodstream, and with a sinking feeling, I realized how much trouble we were in. Goblins were nothing to contend with one on one, but a horde of them might kill us if we didn't finish them off soon.

"There's another group coming!" I cried over the cacophony of sound, slicing my way through two more goblins. "Fall back!"

Kai and the human broke away from the fight, darting to the back wall with myself and our companions. We huddled together against the exit, watching as the handful of remaining goblins tried to reform their ranks. A burst of icy cold shot past my head as Torval lowered his staff once more. In a flash, the remaining creatures were frozen solid, their forms falling to the ground and shattering into a million pieces.

"I don't have any more big spells left in me," Torval gasped, his hands shaking from the strain of his magic. He tapped his staff on the floor twice, five orbs of orange light appearing above it. "This is all I have left."

"Keep out of range," I replied, yanking the arrows from my arm and thigh. "Their arrowheads are poisoned."

The moment the words left my mouth, the human man beside me collapsed, his sword clattering against the stone. His companion knelt down, crying out as she shook him to try to get him to wake up. Dante pushed me aside, drawing his crystalline wand. He placed the sharp tip on the man's chest and muttered a few words under his breath. A warm golden light swelled at the point where the two touched, a moment later seeping into the man's body. His chest heaved as he took a deep breath, but he remained on the ground.

"He'll live," Dante said to the woman.

She forced a smile, giving him a small nod. Reaching under his armpits, she dragged the body back behind the rest of us, propping her partner up against the wall. She gathered up her bow and nocked another arrow, ready to fire from behind us.

"You two!" Dante barked, pointing at the ground in front of him. "Come here!"

I scoffed but stepped up to the cleric alongside Kai. Dante lifted the wand into the air, making a wide circular motion with it, the strange language of magic rolling off his tongue. The air around us crackled with energy, growing warm like we were under the noonday sun. The heat seeped into my body, and I felt the pain ebb away. Glancing down, I watched as the wound on my thigh began to knit closed. The thrum of the poison lessened for a moment, and I felt myself breathe easier. It wasn't gone, but the damage it had done was partially healed, granting me more time.

Looking up at Dante, I felt a sense of gratitude toward him that I didn't think possible. For all the shitty things the clerics did, I couldn't deny their magic was powerful and wondrous. I'd never experienced anything like it before.

"And you," Dante added, pointing his wand threateningly at me, the tip of it digging into my chest. "Keep me safe."

Another glowing ball of light, this time a reddish gold, burst between us. Golden tendrils snaked across my body and armor, pulsing with warmth. Suddenly I felt stronger, faster, and more indestructible. But there was something else there, too, a connection to Dante that I'd never felt before. It was almost like our bodies had been linked together somehow. I could feel his racing heart, the cold fear in the pit of his stomach, and the anxiety in his mind. It was unnerving to feel him so intimately, but I couldn't deny how good it felt to be close to him.

"What is this?" I asked, looking down at the tendrils crawling over my body.

"The blessing of the Twilight," Dante replied. "The connection will allow me to heal you and protect you as we f–"

An arrow slammed into Dante's left shoulder, the force of it nearly knocking him off his feet. My wolf reflexes allowed me to catch him before he hit the ground. I glanced down at the arrow sticking out of his flesh, the black shaft twice as thick as anything we'd seen so far. There was a sticky tar-like substance holding thick black feathers to the shaft, but no hint of the fungal poison I'd seen so far.

Turning back toward the cavern, I saw another ten goblins step through the entrance, their chittering cackles filling the space. They waved their rusty swords and clubs threateningly, trying to strike fear into our hearts. However, that wasn't what worried me.

Behind them, coming into the light, was a goblin nearly three times the size of the rest. He stood easily seven feet tall, his form hunched and bulbous. Thick leather armor was strapped across his figure, and a wicked-looking spear across its back. The head of the spear was rusted, dripping in a thick purple substance that I could only assume was more poison. In its hand was a tall black bow, the other already pulling up another arrow and resting it against the string. I watched as it pulled the arrow back, aiming for Dante once more. I felt the pain and fear rush through Dante's body, our magical connection forcing his sensations into my psyche.

And that's when I snapped.

Nine: Ronan

My sword clattered to the ground as a red-hot sensation filled my body. I felt fangs fill my mouth, claws extend from my fingers, and my bones cracking as my form shifted. At the same moment, I heard the twang of the large bow again, an arrow whistling through the air toward an injured Dante on the ground. With reflexes as fast as lighting, my claws snapped out, snatching the shaft out of the air. It snapped easily between my furry and clawed fingers. My head whipped toward the goblin, a vicious growl echoing out of my throat.

"Don't you *fucking* touch him!" I screamed, using my body as a shield over Dante. I glanced back at Dante, seeing the fear in his eyes. "Stay," I growled, baring my teeth. "I'll take care of it."

Kai stepped up next to me; his hammer gripped in his hands. "I'll take the little ones," he said. "You get the big guy."

I nodded, turning my attention back to the goblins. Rearing back, I let out a furious wolf cry, my roar echoing off the stone and filling the cavern. Several of the smaller goblins took a step back, scrambling at the sudden appearance of a monster in front of them. Their leader, however, didn't budge. Instead, he drew another arrow and placed his aim on me. I didn't move a muscle, staring him down as I waited for him to make the first move. The seconds slowly ticked by, the smaller goblins growing impatient. At last, one of them broke ranks, rushing toward us with all his might. And that's when the arrow flew.

I swiped my clawed hand through the air, intending to break the shaft before it reached me. But I was too slow. I felt the arrow thunk into my chest, sinking in a couple of inches. Dante cried out behind me, the burst of pain affecting us both due to the bond. I grasped the arrow and yanked it free, throwing it to the ground. Together Kai and I rushed toward the goblins.

The one in front was an easy kill, smashed under Kai's hammer. I cut through two more with my claws, their flesh tearing easily under my touch. The leader threw his bow to the side, reaching back to draw his spear. At the last moment, I leaped over the smaller creatures and crashed into their leader, raking my claws down his body.

The sound of tearing leather and howls of pain filled the cavern as we both tumbled to the floor. I rolled off of the rotund creature, coming back to my feet with my claws dug into the stone. Glancing down, I noticed that my arms had elongated, my flesh turning a dark gray as fur sprouted from my pores. My body swelled, straining against the fabric of my clothing and my leather armor, but it didn't break. Both had been constructed by the Brotherhood, taking such transformations into account. In front of my eyes, I watched as my snout grew, my lips curling back to reveal rows of sharp canine teeth. I didn't have to reach up to know my ears had also shifted because I could hear every heartbeat in the room. My senses heightened, and I could suddenly smell the fear in the room as my transformation completed.

It was the first time any of them had seen a monster like me.

But my wolf brain didn't care. All I cared about was protecting Dante, the bond still tethering us together from across the room. My hatred toward him was completely forgotten. His pain was fresh in my mind, and I never wanted that to happen again. He was going to be safe. Even if I had to rip out every goblin's throat I could get my fangs around.

The goblin leader slowly got back to his feet. He reached back, grabbing the spear strapped to his back. But when he pulled it forward, only the top half came loose. He stared at the splintered wood of the shaft, having been crushed beneath his girth. With a low growl, he chucked it away, instead baring his cavity-riddled fangs in my direction. Even without a weapon, he'd be a formidable foe. Behind him, Kai continued to cut down the other goblins, their attacks rendered useless by his sheer strength.

Instead of rushing me, as I expected, the goblin leader reeled back his fist and spun on his heel. Before I could react, his massive fist collided with Kai, sending him sprawling across the cave. He crashed into the stone floor; his hammer left behind amongst the goblin bodies. The leader bent down and scooped it up, blood dripping from the metal head. His mouth spread into a toothy grin as he looked my way, pleased with himself for being so clever.

The rage in my blood threw caution to the wind, and I rushed him, claws held high to tear his eyes out. But he was faster than I thought. The hammer came whistling through the air, the heavy metal connecting with my right arm and lifting me off my feet with a sickening crunch. A yelp escaped my lips as I was tossed sideways, crashing into a stalagmite and sliding to the ground. The moment I came to a stop, I knew my arm was broken.

My lips curled back into a vicious snarl. He'd seen me wield my sword with my right arm, so he took it out before I could get a good hit on him. The leader was much smarter than I gave him credit for. I wouldn't make that mistake again.

Pushing myself back to my feet, I felt the bond between Dante and me suddenly surge with heat. A warmth, like a bonfire on a cold night, spread over the skin on my right side, coalescing around the break in my arm. I felt a sudden shift of bone as it snapped back into place, the intense pain fading. Wiggling my fingers, I flexed my arm. It still hurt like a motherfucker, but it no longer felt broken, just terribly bruised. Still, it was enough to put me back in working order.

I glanced behind the goblin, seeing Kai still lying unconscious on the ground. Torval was using the last of his magic to pick off the smaller goblins while the human woman fired arrows alongside him. They seemed to be taking care of it. However, as I looked again, I realized I couldn't see Dante. He'd healed me via our connection, but he was out of my sight. Where had he gone?

The goblin leader raised Kai's hammer once more. With a cry of fury, he rushed in my direction, reeling back with the intention of taking my head clean off my shoulders. But this time, I was ready. I held my ground until the last moment before I ducked aside. Above me, I felt the impact of the hammer striking the stalagmite, stone chips flying in all directions. At the same time, I drove my claws forward, plunging my hand deep into the goblin's rotund form.

A cry of pain met my blow, and I felt the hot warmth of blood running down my arm as I removed my hand from his body. However, the blow only seemed to anger him more. His fury grew as he swung the hammer over and over again, each time intent on crushing me to dust with a single blow. I managed to dodge the first, second, and third attacks, taking an opening to slash my claws across his chest. Blood flew in all directions, filling the cavern with its metallic scent. But still, the goblin continued to fight, his movements seemingly spurred on by my attacks.

Another rake of my claws caught him off guard, and he swung high. With a sickening thud, I caught the head of the hammer only inches before it struck me in the skull. For a long moment, we fought, muscles bulging and veins popping in our respective bodies. I felt the sweat pouring down my body. My muscles were quickly losing strength as the poison began to take effect at last. Somehow the massive creature was still going, even with a hole in his belly the size of my forearm. Dark blood poured out of the wound, but I was the one that was about to fall. The others were still preoccupied with the smaller goblins, and I knew nobody was coming to save me. Another push forced me down to one knee, the hammer shaking over my head. I was running out of time.

All at once, the pressure behind the hammer let up, my muscles thanking me for the sweet relief. I glanced up at the goblin, trying to see what had caused him to stay his attack. What I saw was horrifying.

The creature's skin had turned from gray-green to a purplish black. Dark veins spread over its body, a putrid pattern of necrosis. His eyes rolled back in his head as foam spilled from his mouth. The blood that had been pouring out of his body turned black, the smell shifting from metallic to putrid in an instant.

    Before I could process what had happened, the hammer slipped out of my grasp, it and the goblin leader fell to the side with a loud clang. Behind him stood Dante, his crystalline wand outstretched, the tip of it glowing black. He stared at me for a long moment, his chest heaving from exertion. I felt the bond between us shiver and break, the magic fading into nothing. At the same moment, I watched as he sank to the floor, his eyes closing as he crumpled on the stone.

    With the threat gone, I felt the shift fade away, taking all my energy with it. Poison pulsed through my body, and my head spun. I looked down just in time to see the ground rushing up to meet me, the darkness taking me into its cold embrace.

Ten: Ronan

"Hey? You okay?" I heard a gravelly voice say.

A moment later, my eyes opened, the darkness fading at last. I looked up at a stone ceiling covered in stalactites, their sharp tips pointing down at me threateningly. To my left, I saw a green face, tusks protruding from his bottom lip. It was Kai, and he looked beat to shit. He was nursing a black eye, several bruises and small cuts littering his body.

"The fuck happened to you," I groaned, pushing myself up on my elbows.

"You should see the other guys," he smiled. "They look worse."

I turned my head to the side, seeing the dozens of bloody goblins' bodies strewn across the cavern. Kai was right. They *did* look worse.

"Here," he said, holding out a hand.

I took it, allowing him to help me to my feet. My head was still spinning as the exhaustion seeped into my bones. Poison usually didn't take me out, but it left me feeling like shit for several hours afterward. I glanced down at my right arm, taking stock of the massive purple bruise that had formed. It might not be broken anymore, thanks to Dante, but it still hurt like hell.

"Dante..." I whispered.

Kai raised an eyebrow in my direction.

"Is... Is the cleric all right?" I corrected, shaking my head.

"He's breathing," Kai replied, gesturing toward a body lying a few feet away.

I glanced over the room, taking stock of the damage. The goblins were all slain, their leader lying in a giant heap on the ground nearby. The human woman and her partner were near the wall on the far end of the room, Torval kneeling next to them and tending to the man's wounds. Dante was a few feet away; his unconscious form dragged off to the side by Kai, I assumed. I crossed the cavern over to him, kneeling down at his side. Reaching out, I instinctively brushed the blond hair out of his face. He really was angelic.

And he'd saved my life.

"No idea what he did at the end there," Kai said, stepping up beside me. "There was jus' this big ball of black energy, and then *poof*, goblin down."

"Odd," I replied, still staring down at him. "I've never heard of a cleric using damaging magic before. Usually, they just let other people do their dirty work."

"I haven't had much experience."

"Unfortunately, I have...." I turned to look back up at Kai. "Gather the others; we push ahead to find a place to rest."

He nodded. "Right."

I watched him turn back to the others, the four of them putting themselves together enough to travel. Everyone was exhausted, the human man most of all. I turned back to Dante in front of me, savoring the peace on his face while I could. When he woke up, he wouldn't be so gracious, even though I'd saved his life. The Brotherhood was feared, especially by those in power. Doubts were already forming in my mind about getting paid should the mission prove successful. The clerics had a tendency to hunt my kind down, not dole out gold to us. Once he woke, we'd be mortal enemies again.

And yet, as I gathered his light form up in my arms, I couldn't help but remember the bond he'd made between us. With the magic gone, I felt empty, aching for his consciousness near my own. There was something about it that had felt so right, even if every bit of logic in my brain revolted against the idea. And yet, I couldn't shake the empty feeling in my heart that I didn't understand. Even just touching him caused a stirring in my nether regions that sent shivers up my spine. I wanted to touch him, to lean down and kiss his soft lips.

I shook my head. First off, he was unconscious, so that seemed wrong. Secondly, he was a cleric, and in an hour or so, when he woke up, he'd probably try to kill me. It would be best if I just left him behind to be eaten by whatever came along next. But we needed him to finish the job and collect our pay. Maybe I could convince him that what he saw was some sort of magic spell from Torval. He'd back me up.

It was a bad plan, but it was all I had. Only time would tell what would happen.

Two hours later, we found ourselves huddled around a small fire, summoned up by Torval without the need for wood or fuel, the last of his magic for the day. It filled our tiny corner of the cavern with warmth and light, allowing us to rest and recover from the battle. All the others were asleep since I'd taken the first watch. I sat at the edge of the alcove, the long mine shaft falling away into the darkness in front of me. In the distance, I could make out a faint blue glow of crystal veins in the walls, but we hadn't gone much further to explore. Everyone was too tired, and each new turn brought the chance of further danger. We'd decided to bed down before we ran into something we couldn't handle.

Everything so far had been quiet, not a single sound echoing down the stone walls since the goblins had attacked. It was hard to keep myself awake with the warmth of the fire, but I'd let them sleep for a couple more hours before I woke Kai to take his shift. He was the only other one capable of defending himself should something sneak out of the darkness and try to attack us. The human man was still too drained from the poison, and his partner was unwilling to leave his side. Torval was exhausted as well, while Dante still lay unconscious near the fire. I was starting to get worried he might not wake up. Mages were strange, their powers mysterious, and sometimes magic took its toll, bleeding the mage of their lifeforce should they push things too far. And there was a good chance Dante had overextended himself.

I turned back to look at him once more like I had done every few seconds since the others had gone to sleep. For some reason, I was worried about him, and it annoyed the piss out of me. That bond he'd created between us wore off the moment he went down, but the lingering effects were maddening. Had I known that it would cause such a strange pull toward him, I would have told him to fuck off.

I glanced down at the bruise on my arm that had already started to fade thanks to my wolven healing. Then again, the only reason I'd been able to continue fighting was because of his blessing. He'd healed my broken arm in an instant, the rush of magic saving my life. I laughed to myself. To think, a wolf like me would be blessed by a cleric. It seemed like such an impossible thing, and yet... It happened.

My ears perked up as I caught the sound of movement. Pulling my eyes away from the dark tunnel, I turned back to the fire. There, sitting up on his elbows and staring in my direction, was Dante, his blue eyes shining in the firelight.

Eleven: Dante

"You..." I muttered, my voice weak. "You're a... a...."

"A what?" he asked, one eyebrow lifted in my direction.

"A monster," I finished breathlessly. "An unnatural beast."

I glared at him with every ounce of hate I could muster. The things I'd seen during the battle... what I'd *felt* over the bond formed between us... it was unlike anything I'd ever experienced. I'd never felt so much rage and anger in my life. That, coupled with the animalistic urge to maim and destroy, made it almost impossible to fathom. And yet, underneath it, all was something I feared even more.

He'd been *protecting* me. That thought alone made my heart flutter, and that scared me more than anything. Not only was I grateful, but something inside me had awakened, something I didn't want to ever find its way to the surface.

"I'm a werewolf, yes," he replied with a nod. "But not a monster."

"All you beast people are monsters," I spat back, remembering everything I'd been taught by the Masters. "You're all abominations in the eyes of the Goddess of the Twilight!"

"Abominations your order thought was just fine to take a job they didn't want to deal with themselves. The ones they trusted to protect your life." He shot me a long stony stare. "Those *monsters* saved your life today. Without them, you'd be charred meat in a goblin's stomach right now."

I didn't reply but merely glared in his direction.

"None of us mean you any harm. In fact, we want to finish this job as quickly and painlessly as you do. So try to show a little decency."

I pushed myself to my feet shakily, knees knocking together as I tried to stand to my full height. "I won't be lectured by a beast!"

"No, but you'll allow yourself to be saved by one, won't you?"

"Fuck you."

I braced myself against the wall, pushing my way down the hall away from the small, conjured fire. In the distance, I could just make out a faint blue light. Maybe I could find some shelter there, a place to recover away from all these *beasts* that could snap and kill me at any moment. But, more than anything, I needed to get away from him.

"You should stay here," he called after me. "We don't know what's out there. Goblins live in tribes, so there could be more just around the bend."

"Fuck off," I snarled under my breath, pushing my way further down the hall.

I couldn't be around him or the others anymore. This job had proven to be too much for me. Not only was I now drained of power, having pushed myself to the brink of death, but now I knew the truth. Orcs and Draak were one thing, but werewolves were another. Their curse could be passed on, and usually, it killed the receiver. However, the full moons were even worse. I'd heard tales of their kind slaughtering entire villages in a single evening, ripping down doors, and devouring babies in their cribs. And it wasn't just werewolves. All shapeshifters were the same. The moon affected them all, and their change came with an insatiable hunger.

I'd felt that fury, that hunger through the bond when Ronan shifted to protect me. But thankfully, it had been aimed at the goblins and not our party. Had the tables been flipped, we would probably all be dead, our bodies in ribbons on the cavern floor.

And yet, knowing all the horror that could have befallen us, I couldn't help the feeling of being drawn to him. The blessing bond had been strong, so much more than anything I'd ever accomplished before. It was like he was... *inside me*... and without him there, I felt empty. For once, I was glad of my weakened state. Should I have my full power and still feel this way, I might have recast the spell. I knew I was attracted to him, but it was purely physical. It had to be. This was something else, something I didn't understand, and I needed to be rid of it. My only choice was to get away from him, to create some distance so I could think clearly.

Suddenly I felt myself shift to the left, the wall I'd been using for support disappearing from under my hand. I managed to catch myself before I could fall, the stone digging into my knee as it slammed into the ground. Hissing through my teeth, I looked up, trying to figure out what had happened.

My breath caught in my throat as I realized the mineshaft had fallen away, opening up into a massive natural cavern bathed in blue light. I stared open-mouthed as I kneeled at the edge of a massive underground lake, the waters so still they created a perfect mirror of the ceiling above. In the reflection, I saw massive spikes of blue, glowing crystal jutting down. They came to sharp points, each of the pillars at least thirty feet long and several feet wide. In an instant, I realized why the nobles were so keen to get the mines cleared. The magic contained within a single pillar of crystal would be enough to raise an entire fleet of airships that used the crystal as an engine. The Baron stood to become the richest man in all the world should he get his workforce into the cavern.

Pushing myself back to my feet, I headed inward, searching for a small alcove to rest in. I found one only a few yards in and shuffled toward it. In the process, I managed to kick over a large stone, the impact crunching my toes through the leather of my boots.

"Fuck!" I snarled, hopping up and down.

Not only did my foot hurt like a motherfucker, but the arrow wound in my leg had torn open as well, fresh blood spilling down my leg. Hobbling over to the stone, I pulled open my leg bag and plunged my hand in, willing the wand to come to me. I felt the cold crystal touch my palm and pulled it out. Taking a deep breath, I placed the point of it on my thigh near the wound and closed my eyes, trying to draw out some small amount of power to stitch the flesh back together.

"Dante?! Are you o–"

My eyes flashed open, and I looked up just as Ronan came running into the cavern behind me. He had his sword drawn as if ready to fight. Stopping in his tracks, he stared out across the vast underground lake, taking in the scene around him. The expression on his face was one of surprise and wonder, just like it had been for me. Being a mercenary, I figured he'd seen his fair share of beauty in the world, and this place would be no different. But he looked like a child for a moment, enraptured by the natural artistry in front of him.

Maybe we weren't so different after all...

The wand in my hand flashed and sputtered as the half-formed magic tried to take effect but to no avail. I was still wounded and very much in pain.

"Fuck!" I cursed in frustration, nearly throwing the wand to the ground. Instead, I pulled open my leg bag once more and shoved it inside, the wand disappearing inside the far too-small space. "Goddess of the Twilight," I muttered, pointing a finger toward the ceiling. "Why do you abandon me in my time of need?"

"You know the gods aren't real, right?" he said, letting his sword fall back to his side. "They can't hear your prayers." I turned to face him, giving him the dirtiest look I could muster. "Even if they could, they probably wouldn't care."

"Just because the gods turn their backs on monsters like you doesn't mean they've abandoned their devout followers. I *live* with proof of the Goddess every single day of my life. My magic doesn't come from nothing, you know."

"Right," he nodded, slamming his sword into its sheath. "Well, don't let me stop you then. Please, pray until your wounds are gone. Let's see how that goes."

I scoffed, lifting my nose into the air. "I just need to rest," I hissed, crossing my arms over my chest like a petulant child. "My magic just needs time to recover."

"In the meantime," he replied, pulling his satchel out from behind him. "Let me take a look at your wounds."

"Don't you fucking touch me!"

"It needs to be tended to. The last thing I need is your leg getting infected. We don't need any dead weight on this trip."

"Fuck off!"

"Look," he said, stepping up in front of me. "I don't give a fuck what you think about me or my kind or all those people in the other room. But if you can't walk, we'll leave you behind, and then you'll be eaten. I'm sure that's not the ending you're looking for."

"What guarantee do I have that you won't just leave me behind anyway?"

He shrugged. "None. And if you keep being such an insufferable prick, I might just leave you behind anyway."

I glared at him with all the venom I could muster.

"So you've got nothing to lose by letting me patch you up."

The hulking man in front of me stared me down for a long moment, a grin pulling at the corners of his mouth. Apparently, he thought it was funny that I stood my ground against him, finding me to be no threat at all. While I was easily a foot shorter than him, that didn't mean I was a fucking pushover. But at the same time, I had to force down the urge to smile along with him. His grin was almost contagious. Not to mention it made him even more handsome the way it made his eyes sparkle in the crystalline light.

I wanted to shake the feeling away, but as he stepped closer, his scent washed over me. He still stank of leather and sweat, but that spice underneath came through once more, making my legs feel like jelly as he kneeled down in front of me. Suddenly images of him reaching up and wrapping his thick arms around me penetrated my mind. I could see him peeling off my acolyte robes, the cold air causing goose flesh to erupt across my skin. What would his kisses feel like on my neck? His hands grasping at my hips? Would a finger trailing down my torso send me into the throes of ecstasy? Or would it take something more... something bigger that I knew he had hiding in those leather breeches of his...

"So," he said, giving his head a small shake as he looked up at me. "Are you going to let me help you or what?"

Was it just me, or did that look in his eyes seem like he was having similar thoughts? I did my best to glare back at him, trying not to give myself away. Somehow I still felt like I failed.

"Fine," I snapped. "But make it quick."

"Don't worry," he replied with a sneer. "I want to spend as little time with you as possible. But more than that, I don't want to have to carry your sorry ass if this wound gets infected."

I crossed my arms even harder, furrowing my brows.

And the fucker chuckled at me again. "You gonna sit down or what?"

Twelve - Dante

Ronan finished wrapping the bandage around my leg, tying it off tightly so that it kept constant pressure on the wound. It only needed to last until morning when I could heal himself. *If* my magic returned, that was. Everyone knew I'd overexerted myself, and magic was finicky. It could come back overnight, in a day or two, or not for several months. The clerics were trained to avoid such things, but in cases of emergency, the rules went out the window.

"Is that too tight?" he asked, his hands still holding the bandaging.

I winced. "No. It's fine."

He sighed, letting the dressings loosen slightly. "You know, you can just say it hurts. It's not hard."

"Right. Because admitting weakness to a creature like you really makes me feel safe," I scoffed. "I don't know why you're helping me. You'll probably turn on me and rip my throat out before this trip is over."

"You keep talking about my hands or fangs on your throat," he replied with a sly grin. "I'm starting to get the idea that you just want me to choke you a little bit."

I glared at him, my eyes full of rage.

"I've heard that you clerics are so hard up in that sanctuary that you get into some kinky shit. No judgment from me, though. I like a good choke now and then."

"You're disgusting," I spat. "I'd never do anything with a creature like *you!*"

"Who said it had to be with me?" He stuffed the spare bandaging back in his satchel, tucking it off to the side. "You're the one that keeps suggesting it, not me."

"I... I d-did not!" I stammered.

"It's okay. You're not the only one." He pushed himself back to his feet, dusting off the front of his leather trousers, a finger lingering too long on his bulge. "It's the wolf pheromones. They get to everyone."

"I told you, I don't want *anything* to do with you!"

"Whatever," he shrugged. Teasing him was bringing me far too much enjoyment. "I'll leave you to your own fantasies. Just let me know when you need to get dicked down."

"Fuck you!"

"Actually," he said, swooping down in front of him and grabbing him by the chin. "It would be me fucking *you*."

I felt the anger flush across my skin, my cheeks heating up as I stared down at the cocky smile in front of me. But just as soon as I felt it flare up, it faded away, leaving a sense of longing in its place. My gaze flicked from Ronan's eyes to his lips, then trailed down his body. When I looked back up, he had a single eyebrow arched in my direction. He knew something was up.

"So, what was that bond you created between us," he asked, pulling away from me. "I've never experienced anything like that before."

I breathed a sigh of relief at the change of subject. Shaking my head, I tried to put back on the grumpiest look in my arsenal. I needed to keep my distance from this beast. Just because he was *ridiculously* hot, that didn't mean I needed to be so fucking obvious. Besides, he didn't deserve the attention. The guy was a total asshole.

"It's called the Blessing of the Twilight," I replied, turning my gaze down to my leg, attempting to stretch out the pain radiating down it. "It binds the caster and the target together, creating a bond that magic can flow between. Usually, I'd have to touch you to use my healing powers, but the blessing allows it to happen from afar."

"What about the other sensations?" he asked. "It was almost like I could feel your pain as if it was my own when you got struck by that arrow. I nearly brought me to my knees."

The idea of Ronan on his knees in front of me definitely got my mind going.

"I... I don't know what that was," I replied, turning away from him. I couldn't look at him anymore. My trousers were already tented, my cock pulsing under the fabric, and my mind just kept betraying me. "That's never happened before."

"Could you feel my pain too?"

I was quiet for a long moment, not sure if I should let him know the truth. Not only did I feel his pain, but everything else too.

"I... I felt the beast inside you... the one you let loose."

The part I didn't tell him was how much it excited me. The rush of adrenaline and animal instinct was intoxicating, something that I found myself craving once more. For that brief moment, I'd felt so powerful, much more so than I ever had in my own body. Magic was one thing, but the ability to protect yourself with only your bare hands? Well, that was something incredible and not common in my order. Not only that, but I felt his overwhelming urge to protect me like I was the most important thing in the world to him. I didn't quite understand why he felt that way, but I was drunk with it. I'd never felt so wanted in my entire life. The only question was, once the beast was gone, did the feelings remain?

"Did... Did you feel anything else?" he asked timidly.

I paused for a long moment, the truth nearly slipping off my tongue. "N-No... Of course not. Nothing at all."

Ronan's eyes darkened as he read the expression on my face like an open book. He kneeled down on the ground in front of me, placing both his hands on my thighs. Leaning close, a deep growl vibrated through his chest, his lips brushing against my neck.

"You're a bad liar," he whispered. His tongue flicked out under my ear, the wet heat giving me goose flesh across my entire body. "Feel anything now?"

"W-What... What do you w-want from m-me?" I managed to force out, my hands gripping the stone so hard I thought it would shatter.

"The same thing you want," he cooed, nipping at my ear. "I know you feel this bond between us, this *pull*." He leaned back, pressing his forehead against mine, his hand on the back of my neck. "You and I... we're enemies. Opposite sides of a war that has been raging for centuries. But you... you're different. I can feel it." His eyes lifted to mine, their dark brown replaced with vibrant gold. "I... I want you."

"I can't...." I began. "We shouldn't...."

He placed his hands on either side of my face, gazing at me with those mesmerizing golden eyes. "Your secret is safe with me."

Something inside me snapped. In the space between heartbeats, my lips were on his, my arms thrown around his neck, the ravenous creature inside of me taking control. It had been a long time since I'd been with anyone, and something about Ronan was driving me wild. I didn't know if it was his wolf side, the fact that he was off limits, or that rich, spicy scent of his that seemed to seep into my pores and fill me up with warmth, like hot tea on a frigid winter's night. I wanted him. All of him. And with the floodgates thrown wide, I could do nothing to stop myself now.

Ronan felt my eagerness, and his kiss intensified, his tongue forcing its way between my lips. His passion drove me wild, the heat of his skin flaring as he swirled his tongue around mine. My hands began to move on their own, running down his body, nothing separating us but thin fabric and a handful of buttons. Thick swirls of chest hair slipped through my fingers, his body hard and powerful beneath my delicate cleric hands. He was everything I wasn't, and I couldn't get enough of him. Before I knew it, I'd undone all of his shirt buttons, tearing at the fabric to release him at last.

With a cocky chuckle, he pulled away from me, taking only a moment to toss his shirt aside. The fabric crumpled on the stone, but my eyes were too fixed on his magnificent form to worry about that. In fact, I didn't even notice him pulling my tunic off until it blocked my view. The moment it was gone, he wrapped his strong muscular arms around me, pulling me close to his chest.

"You are so beautiful," he growled in my ear, placing kisses along my neck. "So soft... so delicate... like a spring flower about to bloom."

My heart fluttered, the butterflies in my stomach racing so fast I thought I would vomit. Why did that sappy shit hit me so hard? I didn't necessarily want to be seen as soft and delicate, but when Ronan said it... well, it was the most wonderful compliment in the world.

"But I can take a beating," I whispered back, placing a playful kiss on his lips. "Don't be too gentle with me."

His eyes widened, the gold growing even brighter. I felt a throb against my belly as his cock jumped to attention at my words. Apparently, he liked that sort of thing. Just wait until he saw what I could actually do. I just hoped I wasn't too rusty with my skills.

"I want to see you," I said, leaning back to trail a finger down his torso. I stopped with it resting on the pulsing bulge in his leather trousers. "All of you."

There was a small whine, almost imperceptible, that escaped from his lips. "Only... Only if I can see you too."

"Deal." I leaned back against the cool stone, putting myself on full display. "But only if you go first."

Another whine and Ronan nodded eagerly, getting to his feet. He reached down, pulling at the buttons on his trousers hastily.

"Not like that," I said, clicking my tongue. "Do it *slowly*."

I watched as a slight reddish tint came to Ronan's cheeks, but he quickly put on a cocky grin to hide it. He took a step back, his fingers working across the leather. Gripping the fly of his pants, he popped the buttons apart one by one. I gazed greedily as more of his tanned skin was exposed, a dark masculine tuft of hair covering his lower torso. I bit my lower lip in anticipation as the last button came free. With a yank of the leather, his manhood came free at last.

A small gasp escaped my lips as I stared at the throbbing cock in front of me. It was easily the biggest I'd ever seen, even for his large stature. However, that wasn't what got my attention. It was different than any I'd ever seen before. At the base of his dick was a thick knot, nearly twice the thickness of the shaft on either side. The rest of it was human enough except for its size and girth. It was impressive, to say the very least, and it left my mouth watering. My first intrusive thought was how I'd manage to fit it inside me.

"You like what you see?" Ronan asked, still grinning.

I nodded stupidly, mesmerized by the throbbing rod in front of me. "Y-Yeah..."

He pressed his finger to the tip, a long trail of glistening precum trailing between them. "You wanna taste?"

I was on my knees in front of him before I could respond, his cock pulsing only inches from my face. His scent was stronger so- close to him, the heat rolling off his body in waves. I took a deep breath through my nose, savoring the spicy smell of his body. Without thinking about it, I leaned forward, my tongue running across the underside of his balls and shaft. At the last moment, I swirled my tongue over his crown, the drop of precum blooming across my taste buds.

"Mmm," I hummed. "You taste amazing."

"Fuck," Ronan growled. "You look damn good doing that." He reached down and cupped the side of my face. "Do it again."

"Yes, sir," I replied, diving back in.

The head of his cock was almost too big to fit in my mouth, and my jaw was pushed to its limits as I tried to stuff the entire thing inside. The sudden rush made me gag, and I had to back off, eliciting a small chuckle from Ronan.

"Don't worry," he smiled. "Everyone does that the first time. Most can't handle me."

He gave me a small wink, and I felt a fire spark in my chest. That was a challenge, and I'd be damned if I was going to fail at something in front of him. Wiggling my jaw to loosen it up, I grabbed the base of his shaft and slipped his crown between my lips, my tongue doing lazy circles on the underside of his cock. A moan and shudder above let me know I was doing a good job. I worked my mouth over him, my hand stroking the parts I couldn't reach. He was too big for me to swallow all of him, and there was no way I was getting over the knot. I couldn't imagine any part of my body that it would fit into, but that didn't take away my curiosity. However, I wasn't sure a cold mineshaft was the place to explore such a thing just yet.

"Fuck Dante," Ronan breathed heavily, moaning with every stroke of my lips. "That feels amazing."

I picked up speed, going faster and faster. I wanted him to burst, to shoot his cum down my throat. That had always been my favorite part back in the temple. The other acolytes were more than willing to acquiesce to my request. I'd been rather popular once in the boys' bathrooms but hadn't had that kind of freedom again for a long time. But at that moment, Ronan was mine, and I was going to get what I wanted.

All at once he reached down and pulled me back, his cock slipping from my mouth with a loud pop.

"Not yet," he heaved, his golden eyes shimmering in the crystalline light. He lifted me to my feet, leaning down to taste himself on my lips. "I haven't seen you yet."

Now it was my turn to be embarrassed. Ronan gave me a little nudge, and I took a step back. After seeing the magnificence of his body, I felt very inferior. Not only was I much smaller than him in stature, but my penis was a normal size. Decent but normal. He dwarfed me in every aspect, and I could already feel the cold creep of self-consciousness up my spine. My face must have given it away, too, Ronan giving me a gentle, encouraging smile.

"Here," he said, kneeling down in front of me. "Let me help."

His massive hands trailed down my torso, his fingers digging in around my hips. He could nearly wrap his fingers completely around my waist, the feeling making me shudder. Every inch of him was so powerful, and knowing that he could overpower me at any moment and take what he wanted was equal parts exciting and terrifying. Yet, for all the horrible things I'd heard about monsters like him, he was awfully gentle.

"By the gods, you're gorgeous," he cooed, his fingers caressing every inch of me.

"I... I don't think-"

"No," he retorted, cutting me off. "I didn't ask for your opinion on the matter."

There was a tiny surge of petulance like I wanted to argue with him as always. But as his fingers found my waistband and a hand slipped inside, cupping my balls, it slipped away. Suddenly I was overtaken with the sensation of having his hands around my cock, the tingles rocking my entire body. My trousers fell to the stone, and I stood there, completely naked, in front of him as he fondled my manhood.

"Fuck..." he breathed, glancing up at me, the excitement clear in his eyes. "Such a beautiful cock." He leaned closer, breathing deeply. "And your scent... it's *intoxicating*."

I'd never had a man say that to me before, but I loved it. The idea that someone so *normal* could excite someone like Ronan... it seemed ridiculous. But as he drew me close, a deep growl of satisfaction vibrating through his chest as his tongue flicked across the crown of my cock. I knew he was telling the truth. Somehow, I could feel just it. At the temple, other acolytes had just been a means of getting off. But Ronan, he was practically *worshipping* me, his face buried in my groin as he breathed me in. He licked across my hips and belly, leaving little nibbles along the way. It was like he couldn't get enough of me, and he hadn't even gotten to the main event yet.

As he pulled back and his eyes settled on my cock once more, I realized he was about to.

Before I could even get a word out, Ronan had swallowed my entire cock down to the hilt.

"Fuck!" I cried out, my voice echoing across the cavern.

I immediately brought a hand to my lips, worried I'd wake the others. Ronan only chuckled, his tongue rolling over the underside of my shaft. He slurped loudly, taking every inch of me over and over again.

"Fuck you taste good," he mumbled before diving back in again.

"Ah! Oh gods... fuck!" I replied.

Ronan was an expert at his craft, more so than anyone else I'd ever met. His lips were tight around my shaft, creating the perfect amount of friction as he slid up and down. Meanwhile, his tongue did an intricate dance against my glans, sending shivers through my entire body with each stroke. One hand gripped my balls, tugging on them softly, the tension heightening all my other sensations, while the other hand reached up toward my nipple, squeezing it gently between his fingers. Each one individually was enough to keep me rock hard, but all four put together at once were making my body sing in a way I'd never experienced before. Not only that, but it was driving me dangerously close to the edge.

"Fuck... Ronan," I gasped. "I'm getting close."

Another growl, the sound vibrating through my cock and driving me even closer. I knew that he wanted me to keep going, to fill his mouth with my seed. Even if I wanted to stop, I didn't think I'd be able to. His hand came away from my chest, plunging down between his legs and gripping his own throbbing cock.

"Oh fuck... I'm... I'm gonna..."

Ronan stroked me faster, his hand pumping between his legs. The sensations were too much, and I rocked my hips forward, my abs tensing. A wave of pure ecstasy flooded my body as I unloaded into his mouth, coming over and over again. He eagerly swallowed my cock down to the hilt, drinking every last drop of my seed.

Within seconds I felt him tense, a few short grunts echoing out of his cock-stuffed mouth. Ropes of thick sticky cum coated the stone floor between us as he shot his load. Finally, he pulled himself away from me, gasping for air. A smile curled across his face as he stared up at me. His tongue flicked out, catching a single drop of cum that had tried to escape. He seemed to savor the taste.

As the waves of pleasure subsided, my senses began to come back to me. There was another flush of embarrassment and then fear as I looked over Ronan once more. I'd been so caught up in the moment that I hadn't realized how much he'd changed. Instead of the human-looking man I'd known before, I saw a partially transformed monster. His ears had become pointed, more hair sprouting along his jaw, arms, and chest. Sharp canines adorned his grin, and I could just make out half-formed claws at his fingertips.

I pulled away from him, realizing what I'd just taken part in.

"Something wrong?" he asked, his head cocked to the side.

"Stay... Stay away from me..." was all I could manage to get out.

"What? What did I do?"

He seemed genuinely confused, but all I could see was the transformation taking place. The last time he'd done that, he'd turned into a killing machine. Was he about to do the same to me? What if I'd gone further with him? Would he have lost control and killed me halfway through?

"This didn't happen," I replied, grabbing my clothing and slowly backing away from him. "I... I'm sorry."

The apology slipped out unexpectedly, but instead of explaining myself or giving him a moment to reply, I just turned and ran, heading back to the others.

Thirteen: Ronan

Morning came eventually, or at least it would have if there was any natural light in the cavern. I woke in the near pitch dark, the others rustling around me as they came to consciousness for the day. There was no way to tell how much time had passed, only that it hadn't been enough, judging by my sore body and the groans from the others.

And yet, the pain wasn't the first thing I thought of. Instead, I pushed myself up on one elbow and glanced over the group. Using the tiny amount of blue glow seeping down the mineshaft, I eventually located Dante sleeping off to one side, away from the others. He was curled up under his dark cloak causing him to blend in with the stone almost seamlessly. I could just make out the slow rise and fall of his form, his blond hair just peeking out from the edge of the fabric. Everyone else was shifting but still down for the moment.

As quietly as I could, I crept across the stone, careful to make sure my boots stayed absolutely silent. Images flashed through my mind of the night before and what it might've become if we'd both been just a little bit braver. A part of me was revolted by the idea of being involved with a member of the Twilight Temple in any way. But there I was, sneaking across the tunnel to check on him.

I took a knee next to him, the leather of my breeches stretching as I leaned down. Grabbing the edge of the cloak as gently as I could, I lifted it. The minuscule amount of light was just enough for my wolven eyes to make out Dante curled up underneath it. He had his hands pulled up under his chin, giving him an almost childlike appearance. I cocked my head to the side, feeling a small smile pull at my features.

There was something about him that was so fragile and delicate. But at the same time, I knew how deeply powerful he was, maybe even more so than me. Acolytes didn't survive training at the Twilight Temple if they weren't strong. Dante had proven himself many times over by mastering his magic and being entrusted with a mission such as theirs. Clearly, he'd done something to garner the attention of the temple masters. That fact alone should have put me more on my guard. A cleric with ambition was a dangerous thing. However, the bond I felt with him had only strengthened since the battle with the goblins. Even though the magic had faded, the connection remained, growing stronger with every passing moment.

I knew that I shouldn't allow myself to feel anything towards him. Sure, he was attractive and definitely my type, but that didn't mean I had to let myself *feel* things. Clerics only cared for themselves. That was the way of the world. Once the job was done, he'd be gone. But a flickering flame of hope had been sparked in me the night before. All those years, I'd been traveling through Eadronem, wishing that one day I'd find the perfect man for me. The elusive *'One'* that everyone was always searching for. I'd slept with a few on the road, had short-lived flings that lasted a few days or a couple of months at the most. Several times I'd bought a courtesan's freedom and sent them on their way to make a new life, wanting more than anything to accompany them and give up mercenary work altogether.

But eventually, they all passed, like dreams forgotten in the drowsy moments just before dawn. And never had I felt a connection deep in my gut like this. Nervous energy? Sure. But never anything *real*.

Until now.

As I stared down at Dante, it began to dawn on me just how much trouble I was in. Already my heart felt as if it no longer belonged to me, clouding my thoughts and judgment. *That* was dangerous. On a mission like the one we were on, a moment's distraction could be the difference between life and death. But as I stared down at that angelic face, the very image of everything I wasn't, I realized it was already too late. He had his claws in me. And the worst part was, I didn't know if it was some magical after-effect or a real connection. Either way, I wasn't able to resist it.

And yet, something the night before had thrown him off. He'd run off in such a hurry, seemingly disturbed by something. I didn't think I'd done anything wrong. Then again, maybe it was just the reality of the situation settling in. He was a cleric, and I was a werewolf. I didn't have anything to lose, and he... well, he'd lose everything if the temple found out.

A sudden groan and shifting came from under the cloak, and I dropped the fabric immediately. With cat-like grace, I dashed back across the tunnel to my original spot and laid down, trying to look like I'd been there all along. What little bit of warmth my cloak had gained in the night left in my absence. Shivering, I pulled it up to my shoulders, my eyes still peering through the dark toward Dante.

He pushed the cloak aside, his blond hair askew from sleeping on it. I could tell from his blinking eyes that he couldn't make out anything in the dark. Humans didn't do well in such conditions. He sat back on his butt, leaning against the wall as he pulled the cloak tightly around his body. Lifting a hand high in the air, he muttered a few words under his breath. Like the glow of a firefly, a soft ball of greenish pulsing light appeared in his outstretched hand. With a gentle nudge, it floated up a few feet, illuminating the tunnel where they all slept.

Dante pulled his hand back into the cloak, glancing over the others that he could see at last. They shifted more in response to the dim light, but it wasn't harsh enough to rouse them from their sleep immediately. I felt a sudden strange pang of gratitude toward the cleric. He could have summoned a holy light as bright as the sun to rouse the others, forcing them to abandon their precious sleep and get back to business.

But he didn't. Instead, he allowed them to slowly wake up, showing a sense of decency that I'd previously thought clerics incapable of. It was a tiny gesture, but one that spoke volumes about the kind of person he was. Despite the terrible things he'd said during our journey, I began to get the feeling that he was merely repeating what he'd been taught at the Twilight Temple without actually believing them.

Maybe... Maybe there was hope for him yet.

Over the next twenty minutes or so, I slowly got up with the others, taking care to make it look like I'd been asleep all along. The last thing I wanted was for Dante to push me away again. We hadn't ended the night previous on the best note, but I wanted another chance at it should we have some privacy, even though I knew that was stupid to do. A part of me still despised the guy, but I was willing to give him a chance to prove he wasn't just some puppet of the master clerics. Maybe if the connection between us was strong enough, he might...

No. I brought my thoughts to a screeching halt. False hope and pining weren't things I did. A life of hardship had taught me that hope was worthless when it came to the harsh realities of the world. And pining after people? Well, that just led to hurt feelings, and I couldn't afford any more distractions in the mines. Not if I wanted to survive. I needed to get him off my mind permanently. He was off limits.

"There's a lake up ahead," Dante said, at last, getting everyone's attention. "We can refill our waterskins there. But be on your guard. We're moving into heavily crystallized sections of the cavern now. Our worm friend could be around any corner." He glanced over at the Draak, giving him a small nod. "Don't use your magic unless absolutely necessary. If we have to face the worm suddenly, we'll be relying on your power the most to take him down."

"Understood," Torval replied, bowing his head.

"There'll be no need for light up ahead," Dante added, pulling his floating orb down closer.

"Why's that?" Kai asked, furrowing his brows in confusion.

"You'll see."

With that, he headed up the tunnel, the glowing orb bouncing over his head as he walked. I followed close behind, with Torval at my back. The human pair stayed in the center while Kai brought up the rear. Everyone was walking a bit slower after the goblin encounters the day before, especially the humans. The male had been the most hurt during the battle, and while he limped a little, it seemed that Dante's magic had done most of the work. In a tight spot, he'd still be able to fight, and that was all I cared about. If the crystal-devouring worm was going to be tougher than the goblins, we'd need every available hand to take it down. I could only do so much, even in my shifted form.

It was only a minute or two before we found the edge of the cavern where Dante and I had met the night before. The others stopped at the entrance, their mouths agape just as mine had been when I first saw it. A vast black lake was reflecting massive glowing blue crystals. It was like a dream, something out of a storybook for children. Even upon a second viewing, I could barely believe my eyes.

"We'll follow the edge of the lake," Dante said after the long silence. "Keep an eye open for any signs of the worm and try to stay as silent as possible. Any sound you make will be carried by the lake across the cavern. We have no idea what might live on the other side." He paused for a moment as if thinking to himself. "Fill up your waterskins, but disturb the water as little as possible."

We all nodded and slowly crept up to the edge of the lake. Pulling out my waterskin, I drained the remaining contents down my gullet before slowly dipping it into the lake. I couldn't help but hiss through my teeth as the freezing cold water enveloped my hands. It was like ice, so much colder than I even thought possible. The cavern wasn't warm by any means, but I couldn't see my breath. However, I had no doubt that should any one of us fall into that lake; we'd succumb to hypothermia in a matter of minutes. Without a fire, even a quick slip would prove fatal.

Thankfully nobody took a plunge, and with our supplies refreshed, we started down the path once more. There was a kind of natural edge to the lake where the stone had been eaten away by the water. I leaned over the edge more than once, trying to peer down into the inky water. But there was nothing to see beyond the perfect reflection of the glowing crystals jutting out of the ceiling. The edge was sheer, that was for certain, but whether it went down a couple of inches or several hundred feet, I couldn't tell. It was a dark void, swallowing every bit of light that touched it.

In places, the path grew thin and precarious, stone walls forcing us to walk paths barely wide enough for a single person to pass. Dante, of course, was in the lead, his glowing orb now extinguished. Our eyes had become accustomed to the glow of the crystals, but it was still difficult to see in places. Halfway across a thin spot, I watched him falter, the path crumbling under his feet and into the lake. He windmilled his arms, trying to right himself, but began to topple over. With lightning-fast reflexes, I caught his arm, yanking his light form back against me.

He clutched my waist, pressing his face against my chest. For a moment, he just sat there, breathing hard. I could feel his heart beating wildly under his ribs. Whether it was from almost falling or from being so close to me, I couldn't tell. However, I felt my hands wrap across his back, my chest rising as I inhaled his soft flowery scent, letting it fill me up. My cock twitched immediately, pressing against the supple leather of my breeches. I still wanted him, and last night had left me more horned up than usual.

His bright blue eyes glanced up at me, a knowing look on his face. He felt the same way, too, and judging by his expression, he'd noticed my growing problem as it pulsed against his belly. His scent shifted instantly, the flowery smell filling with lusty pheromones.

He wanted me too.

"I can walk by myself," he snapped, pushing himself away from me in a huff.

"Doesn't look like it to me," I replied, annoyed that he always put on such a ridiculous attitude. He couldn't hide his true thoughts from my wolven senses. "You nearly went in the water that time, and I don't want to spend the next three hours waiting for you to thaw out."

"Well, maybe if you weren't crowding me so much–"

"You little shit! If I wasn't close, you'd be—"

"Quiet!" Torval hissed behind us. "Listen!"

Everyone stopped dead in their tracks, Dante's mouth hanging open as he readied his next retort. For a long moment, it seemed like Torval had just been trying to shut us up. But just when I thought it was safe to speak once more, I heard it.

A deep rumble echoed through the stones, so light it was almost inaudible even to my heightened senses. It was low and undulating, like a song echoing through the crystals overhead. The vast glassy lake rippled, the perfect reflection marred as the water shifted. Something was in the rocks, and whatever it was, it was *big*.

"What do you think it is?" I whispered, my eyes still focused on the crystalline points jutting out of the ceiling. Should the vibrations knock one loose, we'd all be crushed to death in an instant.

"I believe... it might be... the worm," he replied softly. "It's not in the cavern itself, but it's not far off either."

"What do we do?" Kai asked, looking to me for guidance.

"We can't fight it here," I replied, gesturing down to the thin stone path below our feet. "We'll need a wide open space if we want to take it down. Preferably someplace we can hide and ambush the creature. If we want any chance of defeating it, he can't see us coming."

The rest of the group nodded, all of them staring back at me. I waited for a moment, hoping one of them would have a suggestion. But when none came, I realized I would have to move them forward.

"There," Dante said, his hand pointing out over the lake. "We can attack him from that clearing."

I followed his line of sight to a large open area not too far away. There were several yards of wide open stone pushing away from the lake, creating a stretch of flat stone where we all could fit. On either side, several massive crystalline spikes rose into the air at odd angles. They'd provide enough cover for those of us that didn't fight front and center while also giving us a place to hide until the worm showed up.

On the back wall, I could make out large holes bored through the stone, debris scattered around the entrances like they'd been broken out from the inside. There was damage to the surrounding crystals as well, proving that the worm frequented the area. All we'd need to do is lie in wait to ambush the creature. It might give us just enough of an edge to go home with our heads still attached.

"Lead the way," I replied, nodding in Dante's direction.

For once, he didn't glare at me. Instead, he waved for the group to follow and headed off toward our destination. I just hoped it would be enough to help us kill the worm quickly. Once that was done, I could start focusing on more important things, like Dante's lips and maybe some other places. Neither of us could resist the bond for long.

Fourteen: Dante

The deep rumbling vibrations had continued on and off the entire trek around the lake. I'd moved aside to let Ronan lead the way after a while, the constant slipping and nearly plunging into the freezing cold water putting me ill at ease. Not to mention, I wasn't as physically fit as the rest of the group, and they were growing impatient with my pace. However, even though I could tell he wanted to move faster when Ronan took the lead, he made sure to slow down so that I didn't have to struggle to keep up. At first, I thought he'd make some snide comment about my lack of bulging muscles like his, but he merely offered me silent patience.

It was an odd gesture, and I wasn't sure if I liked it or not. Ever since our little... *interaction*, he'd been almost kind to me. Well, as kind as a grumpy werewolf can be, anyway. He was still surly and rude, but I could tell he was *trying*. I just couldn't understand why.

We both knew the harsh truths of the world. He was a shifter. His very existence was a death sentence in a lot of places. I was a Cleric of the Twilight, an almost noble station that would put me in a position of power for the rest of my life. Our two kinds didn't mix under any circumstances unless it was one hunting the other. I'd admit I had a moment of weakness, his kind words and soft touch drawing up some primal urge within me. In fact, I was still fairly certain my magical blessing on him had caused some unforeseen side effects due to the nature of his being. The strange pull felt between us was nothing more than errant magic and unchecked curiosity. Nothing would ever come of it. Besides, I despised the guy. He was a total prick.

And yet, I couldn't stop myself from thinking about him. His rough hands on my skin, as he bound my wounds, were so gentle and strong, showing me more care and delicacy than I thought possible. When he'd pulled me close, his body pressing against mine, I'd felt so safe and protected, like nothing in all the world could touch me with him around. A part of me wanted him to hold me like that forever, to keep me close in his embrace. Thinking about his lips pressing against mine made me shiver, and not because of the cold. I'd never felt such passion and heat from another person before. Having sex in the temple wasn't uncommon, but it was always cold and distant, a physical need instead of a real connection.

But it wasn't like that with Ronan. When he kissed me, my world melted away. All that existed was him. And when he'd slipped his hands under my robes, well, I'd pretty much given up on trying to resist him at that point. His fingers were digging into my hips, the soft touch of his tongue against my cock.... All of it drove me insane. Then, when he'd released his own... well, let's just say I was mesmerized. I'd never seen anything like it before. Not only was he big to match the proportions of his body, but the thick knot at the base of his shaft and the wide crown of his cock... it drove me crazy in a way that I'd never experienced before. Every acolyte in the temple was human, and it had never crossed my mind that genitalia would be different across other species or with shifters. I couldn't help picturing his throbbing member every waking second since the night before. I'd even dreamed about the damn thing and how good it would feel to climb atop him and ride it. The head would hit all my spots perfectly, but the knot at the base? Well, that might rock my world forever. Or tear me in two. Probably the latter.

I shook my head, trying to drive the thoughts away. If they were just purely sexual, it wouldn't be a problem, but they were bordering on obsession. And, even though I didn't want to admit it, there were emotions behind them. That went against the teachings of the Goddess and my entire order. Attachments were not allowed, and I'd already broken that rule too much just by being friends with Calder. At the rate I was going, the Goddess would revoke my magic completely. The Masters had warned us such a thing might happen if we didn't accept the teachings completely. I'd seen acolytes disappear overnight before, the Masters letting us know the next day that they'd been sent home because their magic was gone. I couldn't risk my entire life on the first asshole that happened to show me the tiniest bit of kindness.

It was pathetic how much I'd grown to want him, especially since he'd been a jerk since the moment we'd met. No, he wasn't worth my time or my interest. I had bigger things to accomplish. And as for his dick... well... he could keep it to himself. I didn't need it!

"You all right?" a gruff voice in front of me asked.

I glanced up, realizing that Ronan was standing only a couple of feet from me, his hand outstretched to help me over a particularly treacherous section of stone. His brows were furrowed together as if he was worried about me.

"Fine," I snapped, ignoring his hand. "I don't need your help either."

The concern on his face melted away into irritation, but he kept his mouth shut. "Let me help you," he offered, reaching out further.

"I said I don't need it!"

I smacked his hand away and scrambled over the stone like a toddler, making an absolute fool of myself in the process. But it didn't matter. I knew I couldn't let him in again, or even close to me for that matter. His touch was too hard to resist once he made contact, so it was best to just avoid him in the first place. My life as a cleric was more important than his temporary affection. Besides, I knew full well what men like him were like. He'd get his piece of ass and fuck off the moment he got the chance. There was no future where the pair of us were concerned, and I liked it that way. I wanted to keep my magic, and I was sure he wanted to keep his hide. Apart, we both got our wishes.

Echoes and vibrations continued to sound from within the stone, but it still seemed a long way off. Leaving the others to fend for themselves, I found a small alcove between the crystalline spikes to be alone for a while. Until the rumbling sounded closer, we had some much-needed time to relax. For me, that meant pulling the wand from inside my bag and finally seeing to the wound in my leg.

The walk for the day had been exhausting, but it had also given me a chance for my magic to recover somewhat. I still didn't feel like I was back to normal, but there was enough stored inside me to see to my leg. The last thing I wanted was to go into battle with a limp. That would guarantee my demise for sure.

Unwrapping the bandages around my thigh, I let them fall to the stone in a heap. With the tip of the wand gently pressed against the wound, I muttered under my breath, calling up the holy magic within me to knit the skin back together. A rush of heat swept across my body, coalescing around the wound, and I felt the uncomfortable wriggle of skin and muscle as they pulled themselves back together at last. The pain finally dulled, letting my senses open back up once more.

I looked down at the wand, feeling the power within me drain away once more. My thumb traced over the facets of the crystal, my mind wandering as I stared. The magic to heal wasn't new to me, the feeling of it more familiar than my own name sometimes. But the magic I'd done against the goblin leader… the *darkness* that took over him… it terrified me. I knew its name, although I didn't know how. It was mostly just a feeling and a few small passages in arcane books I'd read back at the temple.

Necromancy.

The thought of it made me shudder. It was the antithesis of the Goddess of the Twilight and her gifts bestowed to the clerics. The magic came in many forms: raising corpses to fight again, siphoning life and magic off of other creatures, and what I'd done, killing the flesh of another living creature with a simple touch. I glanced down at my hands, half expecting them to be stained black or covered in black veins. Of course, they weren't, but they tingled nonetheless like the magic was waiting just under the surface.

I blamed Ronan for it. The bond shared our emotions across a magical thread, and his fury had driven me over the edge, warping my magic into something I shouldn't have been able to do. Necromancy was forbidden and outlawed across all of Eadronem. There were some who tried to argue that the healing and resurrection of living flesh were the same things, but that wasn't what I'd been taught. To save life was the gift of the Goddess. To destroy it was the realm of the Goddess of the Storm. She too was outlawed, her gifts of destruction and chaos enough to land almost any mage in prison. My eyes flicked up to Torval as he stood conversing with Kai and Ronan. The Draak's magic was no doubt a gift from the Storm, whether he knew it or not.

Had the Goddess of the Storm turned her eye on me, or had the Goddess of the Twilight turned away? I wasn't sure which was the case, but both of them scared me nonetheless. I narrowed my gaze, glaring at Ronan from afar. If he hadn't lost control, I never would have been put in the situation in the first place. It was his fault my magic had gone haywire, clearing under the influence of his monstrosity. It had to be. I knew there was nothing wrong with me because the Masters of the temple would have found it out already and saved me. No, it was Ronan's doing. I was sure of it.

"Are you... okay?"

I spun around, the voice making me startle so hard I nearly dropped my wand. Behind me, I saw the dark-skinned man leaning against the crystal wall, his partner only a few feet beyond. Not wanting to break my only weapon, I slipped the wand back into my bag, the shaft disappearing into the dark depths within.

"Y-Yeah," I replied, surprised by the man's words. I'd been almost certain he didn't speak the common language of Terrastera. "I'm fine."

"Good," he nodded. "You... look uh..." He gestured to his face, making a frightened expression.

"Scared?"

"Ah! Yes."

"I'm not frightened," I replied. "Just thinking."

"Good to think," he nodded again. "Worm soon come. Ready to fight."

"We'll be ready," I said. "Are you feeling better?"

He furrowed his brows, turning toward his partner as if looking for guidance.

"Your wounds," I added, pointing to where the arrow had struck him. "They're healed?"

"Yes!" he half shouted, my message coming through loud and clear. "Much better. Thanks to you and my wife. All better."

"I'm glad to hear it."

"It's hard," he continued. "For people like you and me."

"What do you mean?"

He gestured to the others talking amongst themselves. "They strong. Power of dragon and wolf and orc. Very intimidating." He pointed back to his wife, then to me. "But us only human. Easier to get hurt. To die."

I wasn't sure if I believed what I was hearing. Master Ryker had specifically told me that all the hired people for the mission were monsters. But this man and his wife claimed to be human. They were from another part of the world, to be sure, but not like the others.

"You're... human?" I asked, making sure I understood.

"Yes," he nodded. "My wife is great archer, and I know how to use swords, but no special powers."

"Where are you from?" I asked, my curiosity piqued. "I've never met people like you before."

"We travel far from the south, across mountains and sand," the man replied, his eyes far away as if recalling the harsh memories. "Eadronem is only small part of big world. Much beyond the mountains and across the sea."

"I... I didn't realize there was so much."

"More than any man can see in one lifetime."

I was having a hard time fathoming such a thing. The view from the dormitory windows was expansive, looking over miles and miles of the countryside below the clouds where the people of Eadronem lived. The airship ride had shown me even more, the size of the Soroma Crystal and Aratis showing me just how small I really was. And yet a man now stood in front of me that said the world was even larger, stretching out beyond mountains and ocean to places where other people lived that I'd never even heard of before. The Masters had said nothing existed outside of Eadronem.

The pair gave me warm smiles. Why had Master Ryker lied about them? Why did all of them lie about the world? If they were willing to tell falsities about those things, what else had they filled our heads with that had no base in fact?

Fifteen: Ronan

The day drifted by, mostly in silence. After the initial hustle to get everything in place should the worm appear, things eventually died down, leaving an ear-splitting silence to fill the cavern. Only short bursts of sound, the deep vibrations of the worm some ways off, punctuated the day, bringing sweet relief to my sensitive ears for only a moment. They'd been ringing nonstop since we'd gotten to the underground lake. This deep in the world, there was nothing that could penetrate the rock. The missing rustle of leaves, birdsong, and breeze drove me almost insane. Wolves weren't supposed to be this far underground.

I'd found a place near one of the crystal pillars to settle down for a bit, spreading my cloak over the stone to give me some semblance of comfort. It was still cold and hard, but at least a little less than it would have been normally. However, my place amongst the pillars, diligently chosen, afforded me a good view of Dante. He'd spent a little while conversing with the human pair before settling down in the little nest he'd made for himself. So far, he hadn't spotted me, and I'd grown brave with my blatant stares.

Even after all the time we'd spent traveling and setting up our little ambush, the bond between us hadn't lessened. I could still feel it, like a thread pulling at my chest, trying to convince me to get closer to him. I wanted to touch him, to wrap him up in my arms and kiss his neck, his warmth pressed against my chest. Even from a distance, I could smell him, his light flowery scent stronger than all others in the cavern. But maybe that's because I was looking for it, ravenous to taste him on my lips once more.

Our private moment beside the lake had given me a taste, and I was ravenous for more. His pale lithe form was so supple under my fingers, so easy to manipulate into the best positions. And that look in his eyes... that *hunger*... well, let's just say I needed to see that again. The way he stared at my body and my cock... it was enough to drive any man crazy. I found myself wondering how he'd feel, his tight ass stretched over my thick member. The extra ridges and knot didn't seem to bother him, but whether he could take it or not was a different story. Even the most experienced courtesans had given up, but none of them had that look in their eye as Dante did.

And all that fantasizing was fun, but something was bothering me. I was beginning to *care* about him. Not in the same way as the courtesans I'd freed, but something deeper, like he was pulling at my very core. The bond had deepened my connection to him, and I couldn't deny that I was falling faster than I wanted to. Already his snide comments bothered me less. In fact, I was starting to find them to be kind of cute. The way his brows scrunched up when he got frustrated and the little click he did with his tongue when he didn't agree with someone it was endearing. And that could only spell trouble.

Werewolves and clerics didn't mix. That was obvious. If anyone were to find out my true identity, I could be imprisoned. I was already taking a terrible chance letting Dante know to begin with. Not to mention, the teachings of the Twilight Temple forbade clerics from forming relationships. They could fuck, sure, but they couldn't care about anyone. All the clerics I'd met made it a point to do the exact opposite, in fact. We could never be together, so it made more sense to continue hating him. It would be easier for both of us in the long run.

But I wasn't sure if I could.

Maybe if I just talked to him, one on one, we could get things straightened out. I needed to know how he actually felt about me, and he needed to understand that I wasn't just some crazy beast. At the very least, I needed to be sure that he wasn't going to turn me in the moment we stepped out of the mines.

I glanced around, taking stock of the others. They'd gathered around a small fire that Torval had conjured up near the edge of the lake. All of the lights had been doused, and the dim crystal glow was all they had to go by. If I went now, I could speak with Dante without being seen or overheard.

It was my only chance.

Taking a deep breath, I pushed myself up from my small cove. Grabbing the cloak, I threw it over my shoulders and softly crossed the cavern to where Dante was sitting, not wanting to alert the others to my presence. I'd waited until I was nearly on top of him before I cleared my throat as softly as I could.

There was a flurry of cloak and limbs as Dante suddenly withdrew the crystal wand hidden within the fabric, the sharp end pointing directly at my jugular. He was fast, much faster than I thought possible. Still, with my wolf reflexes, I could have parried it. Probably.

"Sorry," I said, trying my best not to sound as gruff as usual. "I... uh... didn't mean to frighten you."

"Right," he scoffed, pulling the wand back. "You just meant to sneak up on me. I see."

"I wasn't—" I began but stopped myself. Taking a deep breath, I crouched down beside him, trying to exhale the knee-jerk reaction to snap at him. "I wanted to speak to you without the others knowing, so I was trying to be quiet."

His blue eyes glared up at mine, searching for any hint of a lie.

"Why?" he asked simply.

Another deep breath. "Because I wanted to talk about what happened last night. When we were alone."

"Nothing happened," he said quickly, his cheeks flushing bright red even in the dim light of the crystals. "There's nothing between us."

Well, I guess that answered part of my question. Although, judging by how hard he was blushing and the sudden rush of heat from his body, he probably wasn't telling the truth. I could hear his heart pounding in his chest. Obviously, it was still on his mind too.

"Okay," I nodded, trying to let it go. "Then I wanted to talk to you about them," I said, gesturing toward the others. "And myself."

"What for?"

His impatience was getting on my nerves. And, if I was being totally truthful, turning me on a bit. I started to picture him flat on his back, my hand wrapped around his throat. I had a feeling he'd be less likely to talk back with my thick wolf cock shoved up his ass. But then again, maybe he'd be annoying the whole time. Either way, I was weirdly into it. I was growing tired of all those demure courtesans. It was about time to find one that fought back.

"I wanted to advocate for them," I continued, shoving the fantasies away, my leather pants already too tight at the crotch. "Would you agree that they've kept you safe? Even taking wounds to keep you out of harm's way?"

"Yeah," he nodded with a raised eyebrow. "What's your point?"

"I know people like me... like them... well, they aren't exactly seen as 'good' in the eyes of most people. Especially..." I looked up at him, not wanting to say the words but knowing I had no other choice. "Especially to the Clerics of the Twilight."

"Are you suggesting my order is wrong?" His voice rose in pitch as he glared at me. "That the Goddess herself has made a mistake?"

"Do you think these people are bad? Just because of what they are?"

He paused for a long moment, his eyes flicking back and forth as thoughts passed by. To my surprise, he floundered. Clearly, something I said had thrown him off his guard. It wasn't like him to not have a snappy retort.

"I... I don't know," he replied at last. "My master says they're not to be trusted, that they're all monsters."

"Even the humans?" I asked, gesturing toward the pair sitting next to Torval. "Why are they monsters?"

"They... They aren't... but my master said everyone hired would be." He glanced up at me, his eyes full of confusion. "Could they be hiding something?"

"Well, I can assure you that they're only human." I reached up, tapping the side of my nose. "This sniffer never lies. So no, I don't think they're hiding anything. They're definitely not from inside Eadronem, but maybe somewhere else."

"So... So there are lands outside the ring of mountains?"

My jaw fell open. "Of course there are... Did you think we were the only people on this entire planet?"

"That's what I've been taught."

I couldn't believe what I was hearing. Eadronem was only one small section of the world. I'd never been outside of it, but I'd met enough people to know that there was much more to be seen. Hell, even the nobles knew that! They flew their wares all over the world on their airships. How could the temple acolytes not know about that? Did they keep their dogs so chained that they didn't even let them look out the window now and then?

"I'm afraid you've been lied to."

Dante's form immediately stiffened, his muscles tensing as he pulled away from me. The expression on his face hardened, and I realized I'd said the wrong thing.

"My master wouldn't lie to me."

I took a deep breath. "Look, that might be true. And you can believe whatever you want, but I came over here to ask you a simple favor."

"What?" he spat.

"When this is all over, I want you to let these people go. *With* their promised reward."

"Why the hell wouldn't I let them get paid?" he asked, clearly offended. "They're doing the job, and they'll get what they deserve." He pushed himself up from the ground, glaring down at me. "Maybe it's *you* that has some learning to do. Just because I'm a cleric doesn't mean I'm the biggest fucking asshole in the world, you know. Although, it seems you're determined to keep that title to yourself from the way you keep going on."

He made to walk away, but my hand shot out to grab his arm of its own accord. My body reacted so quickly that I barely had time to think. Before I knew it, I was on my feet, pulling Dante close to me, my arms wrapped around him. He struggled to escape my grasp, but his feeble attempts were laughable at best.

"Why do you despise me so much?" I asked softly. "I know you feel it too, the bond between us." I leaned in, my lips brushing across his neck as I breathed him in. "And I know you like me, despite everything you say. You reek of lust and conflict. There's something you're not telling me... or something you don't want to admit to yourself."

"I... I don't know what you're talking about," he said, still struggling. "I don't want anything to do with you."

I lifted him off his feet, pressing him against my chest so that we were face to face. "Is that so, little one?" I could feel his heart pounding under his ribs and the telling throb of his cock against my belly. "It seems you want nothing more than to be close to me. You're practically *begging* for it."

"No I... I don't..."

My tongue was on his neck, his words becoming more stilted by the moment.

"Leave me... I... fuck..."

"You like it, don't you?"

"I... stop..."

"Is that what you really want?"

There was a long pause.

"No."

It was so soft I almost didn't hear it.

"Then tell me what you want."

"I..." he began. "I want you... to... to..."

His words were cut off as a deep rumble echoed through the ground, the crystals around us quaking at their foundations. The telltale cracking of stone pulled my attention upward toward the back wall of the cavern. A massive split had formed in the rock and continued to slowly spiderweb as something from within pushed its way through. The time had come.

I was careful to place Dante gently back on his feet, leaning down to leave a quick kiss on his cheek.

"We'll continue this afterward," I said, pulling my sword from its sheath. "Make yourself ready. The crystal worm approaches."

Dante shook his head, trying to clear his thoughts. Drawing the crystalline wand from his bag, he reached out a hand and placed it on my arm. Muttering under his breath, I saw a light erupt in his palm, the heat of it seeping into my skin and throughout my entire body. All at once I could feel his heartbeat and the adrenaline pumping through his system, but this time it was stronger than before, to the point where I felt as if I could hear his thoughts.

"Goddess of the Twilight be with you," he said. He turned away for a moment but stopped and reached out once more toward me. "I... I don't know what this is," he said. "But I wish... to speak with you more."

"I'll do my best not to die then," I nodded with a cocky grin.

"You won't. I'll make sure of it."

I had to admit that confidence in his voice was sexy. But there wasn't time to think about that as the stone wall began to crumble, the worm forcing its way through. Behind me, I heard the others scramble into place, taking cover before the creature saw us.

The ambush was our only hope to defeat it.

Sixteen: Dante

My hand was still resting on Ronan's arm when the worm broke through the stone at the far end of the cavern. I felt my grip tighten, my fingers digging into his skin. His eyes flicked in my direction for a moment before he turned back toward our quarry. I was glad to be hidden behind the crystal as the massive creature broke through the stone at last, rock and dust tumbling to the ground.

I felt my jaw slacken as I stared at the beast in front of me, much bigger than I'd anticipated. Its head was easily six feet tall, a perfectly circular mouth with row after row of sharp teeth rotating within. There were no eyes that I could see, but that didn't seem to hinder its understanding of the environment around it. With a slow undulation, it began to push its way out of the tunnel behind it, sharp serrations carved into the stone where it had bored its way through. Its body was dark and fleshy, like an earthworm but with deep skin folds every few inches. Along its back were several crystalline spikes that looked as if they'd grown out of the body itself. I watched as it used them to gain purchase on the stone and force itself out into the open air.

Glancing to the other side of the clearing, I saw Torval, Kai, and the pair of humans hunker down. Kai's hammer clinked lightly on the stone, the sound barely audible over the din of shifting stone. Suddenly the worm stopped, its head slowly turning in Kai's direction. There were no eyes that I could see anywhere on its body, but it didn't seem like it needed them. A low growl emanated from its body, the stones vibrating across the ground. The massive body slowly turned, shifting toward the other group and beginning its slow crawl across the open space.

Ronan tensed beside me as the worm approached, coming close to our hiding place as it headed toward the others. The folds of flesh scraped against the crystal spires, the stone creaking under the strain. A series of soft cracks reverberated through the space as the crystal spiderwebbed but held strong. It looked big enough to crush the creature should it fall, if only it would break.

Maybe I could help it along.

Motioning to Ronan to strike the stone, I slapped my hand against the smooth surface, muttering under my breath. The moment the magic left my fingertips, I felt the crystal react, the spell amplifying far beyond my original intention. A sudden heat erupted across my body, the spell twisting in my grasp. Instead of the spell, I'd cast, the crystal seemed to invade my mind, reading my true intentions. The moment it did, I heard a loud crack, a fissure erupting across the base of the spire. All at once, the heat faded away, and I felt myself slip back into my own awareness. I'd never felt anything like it before, but I knew then that the Masters hadn't been lying about one thing. Soroma crystal was dangerous and far more potent than I'd ever imagined.

But I didn't have long to think about it as my senses returned to the scene before me. The worm had stopped, its massive head turning in my direction. A deep guttural cry echoed from its body as it rose up like a cobra, ready to strike with its whirling rows of razor-sharp teeth. It lurched forward, only making it about halfway before another ear-splitting snap rent the air.

Stopping in its tracks, it turned its head upward as the crystal spire slowly leaned toward it. The body shifted suddenly, trying to escape the massive spire. However, as the crystal leaned further, gaining speed as gravity took effect, I knew the worm wouldn't make it. I pulled up my cloak to block myself from the inevitable crash. At the last second, Ronan stepped in front of me, turning his back toward the creature and using his body to shield me from the debris.

With a cry of pain, the crystal crashed down on top of the worm, the rear third of it smashed under the massive stone pillar. Crystal shattered, and flesh liquified under the weight, the sound of blood and viscera splattering across the open cavern. I lowered my arm, peaking around Ronan's muscular form to see the damage. The monster was writhing in pain, trying to yank its body free of the stone, but to no avail. My companions stared open-mouthed from across the cavern, looks of disbelief painted on their faces. In a single strike, I'd managed to wound the creature mortally. It looked like we might not have to fight it after all.

However, my success was short-lived. The crystals along the creature's back began to glow, that same blue light growing brighter and brighter as it spread down its body. The tail was finally pulled free, blood gushing from the wound onto the smooth stone floor. But the moment the light touched it, the bleeding stopped. I watched in horror as the wounds began to stitch themselves closed. The crystals on its back started to shrink, being used up by the magic it was summoning from within its own body. Apparently, the crystal it ingested wasn't just for sustenance.

"Attack it now!" I cried, pushing my way under Ronan's arm. "Don't let it regenerate!"

There was a brief silence followed by raucous cries as the others drew their weapons and sprinted across the cavern. The worm turned toward the noise, rearing back as they approached. A roar echoed from its toothy maw, the earsplitting sound rippling across the lake. Everyone's hands went to their ears instantly, the piercing shrieking enough to burst our eardrums. I watched as only one managed to break through. Kai was still running, barreling toward the creature with his hammer held high, the steel edge glinting in the dim light. He swung downward, his aim true and weighty.

Dark ichor splashed across the face of the crystal, the worm shrieking once more as it reeled back. The break in the sound gave the others the moment they needed to regain their senses. Shaking the sound from their ears, they rushed forward, and I went along with them. Ronan ran at my side, quickly outpacing me as he approached the worm. However, the others made it there before us.

The human man collided with the creature, his sword sinking into the wrinkled flesh before tearing out in a wide arc. His partner quickly nocked and fired two arrows, both striking the beast just above its gaping maw. There was a flash of fire as a beam of red shot into the worm's mouth and exploded, the flash of heat causing the others to throw up an arm to shield their eyes. Ronan followed up next, running his blade down the monster's side until he slid to a stop at Kai's side. I kept to the outside of the ground, staying at a distance to heal anyone who might need it. In a matter of seconds, our group had done massive damage to the creature, with blood and ichor leaking out onto the smooth stone floor. I felt a smile pull at my lips. Our ambush had succeeded.

But then the wounds began to close again, and the worm lifted its head like a cobra, a deep hiss emanating from its throat. I took an instinctive step back as it scanned our group, searching for its first target. Even with its lack of eyes, I could see it turn toward the human man down in front, the sword having just been pulled from its flesh. With a sudden burst of speed, it lurched forward, the side of its head catching the man and lifting him off his feet. I watched in horror as he was catapulted into the air and across the cavern. He struck the flat stone some thirty feet away, his body bouncing twice before it skidded to a halt. A heartbeat passed, then two, but there was no sign of life from him, not even his chest's slow rise and fall. I knew he was dead before I even had a chance to process the thought.

A scream of rage pulled me back to the battle, my eyes darting to the human woman who loosed arrow after arrow toward the worm. Tears streamed down her face as she yelled in fury at the creature. I may not have understood her language, but I could feel her meaning. The man lying in a heap was important to her, a lover or a close relative. She channeled all her rage into her arrows, each one sinking out of sight into the creature's body. As she pulled the last one, I watched the bowstring snap, the arrow streaking through the air. As it flew, it began to glow, a bright white light pulsing at the tip. The worm turned toward her, the arrow shooting into its open maw. A sudden explosion rocked it from the inside, and I watched as parts of its flesh were burned away, cleansed by holy light.

The woman's power was similar to my own. But how could that be?

I didn't get time to think about it as she and the others rushed forward, intent on destroying the creature once and for all. Kai's hammer shattered a handful of its teeth as Ronan's sword plunged into it again. Three balls of fire struck it as Torval tried to flank it from the opposite side. The human woman rushed it head-on, swinging her bow like a sword. Over the bond, I could feel Ronan's heart racing, the fear streaking through his body along with adrenaline. I couldn't believe someone like him could be so scared, but losing one of the group was enough to put everyone on edge.

And the next moment, it got worse.

The worm's wounds were still regenerating. Half of the wounds inflicted scabbed over, the blood no longer flowing from them. A second later, the worm struck again, this time throwing the front half of its body toward the human woman attempting to beat it to death with a bow. She looked up, her face full of fear as she realized she couldn't get out of the way in time. I had to turn away at the last second, the sickening crunch of bones filling my ears as her life was instantly snuffed out.

Two down. Four to go.

The strikes continued, but with fewer people fighting, the worm recovered more and more of its wounds. Kai continued to strike it over and over, his hammer breaking teeth and flesh with every blow. Torval's magic shot across the cavern, each spell a little dimmer than the last. He was running out of steam quickly. Ronan stabbed and slashed repeatedly, trying to cleave the damn thing in two. More than once, I pulsed healing magic across the bond to mend his muscles torn by the exertion. All three of them were tiring out, and still, the worm kept going. It looked terrible, like it couldn't put up with the onslaught indefinitely, but it wouldn't go down without a fight.

It flailed suddenly, its moves more desperate than they had been before. The head turned left, catching Kai in the chest and tossing him to the ground a few feet away. Its tail went right, swiping Torval's legs out from underneath him. At that exact moment, it reared back, ready to strike at a fallen Kai, completely ignoring Ronan's blade.

I couldn't let it kill another one of my team. Not if we wanted to survive. There was only one choice, and this one chance to use my newfound power.

Summoning up the necromantic magic I'd felt before, I rushed across the cavern, my feet barely touching the ground. With the crystal wand extended, I watched black energy fill the facets, spiraling up the wand shaft until it coalesced in a ball of darkness at the very tip. All I had to do was get close enough to touch the creature. The worm turned in my direction, sensing my approach. It redirected its attack toward me, the head lurching in my direction.

The bond between Ronan and I flared.

"NO—"

But it was too late.

A second later, the wand made contact, and I felt a burst of magic rock through the monster before me. It tore through flesh and bone, instantly turning its blood to ash and eating away at the muscle and sinew that held it together. The magic was powerful, and it did the job. I felt the spell take effect, snuffing the very life out of the massive worm.

However, it did nothing to stop the momentum of its body.

As it came crashing down toward me, I simply closed my eyes.

At least Ronan was safe.

Seventeen: Dante

Something heavy struck me, and I was thrown sideways, the wand flying out of my hands as I hit the ground. I heard it strike the cavern floor a heartbeat later, shattering into a million pieces. At that exact moment, I felt the vibrations of the massive worm hit the ground, coming to a rest at last, its heart no longer beating. But there was something wrong. The bond between Ronan and I...

It was gone.

I turned back, a cold fear rushing through my body like a tidal wave. My eyes widened as I saw what I feared most. Ronan was lying on the stone, partially trapped under the creature. But that wasn't the worst part. Several of the giant crystalline spikes had broken off the worm's back.

And one was sticking straight through Ronan's torso, his body pinned to the cavern floor. I scrambled over, my feet slipping across the smooth stone covered in black ichor. Using the blessing, I reached out, hoping it was just a momentary lapse in the magic. But I couldn't find him. There was no sense of emotion or thought, just a cold emptiness. I placed my hand on his still chest, waiting for him to breathe.

But none came.

"No..." I whispered, the shock of the situation settling in. "No, no, no, no...."

A brief thought crossed my mind, wondering why I was so upset about this man I barely knew. But the next moment, it was gone, replaced by fierce determination. I turned toward Kai, who had barely returned to his feet; the hammer abandoned some distance away.

"Help me!" I cried, reaching forward to grab the crystalline spike from Ronan's chest. "Hurry!"

Kai limped over, nursing a leg covered in blood. He stepped over Ronan, placing his hands on either side of the crystal. Together we lifted, our muscles straining with the attempt. But it wasn't coming loose.

"Again!" I commanded.

The orc looked exhausted, but I wasn't giving up yet. We tensed once more, trying to lift the stone free. I gritted my teeth, straining every inch of my tiny body to break it loose. Just when I thought we'd have to give up, I felt a flush of heat around us. Out of the corner of my eye, I saw Torval; his staff pointed in our direction. Tendrils of golden light wrapped around the crystal-like wire, pulling tight against the stone's surface. Power thrummed around us as he called out.

"Pull!"

Together the three of us put every last bit of energy into our task. For a moment, there was nothing, but then I felt the tiniest shift. Pushing my shoulder against the crystal, I heard a sharp crack, and it came free, a gaping hole the size of my head left in Ronan's chest.

Before I had a chance to doubt, I dropped to my knees, placing my hands over his body. I didn't have a wand to amplify my power anymore, but I didn't need it. Grabbing a large shard of the crystal, I held it over him, pouring my intentions into the stone.

"You will not fall this day," I whispered, leaning close to him. "Ronan... return to me."

A brilliant flash of white light filled the cavern, the others backing away with their arms up to shield their eyes. But I didn't look away from Ronan's unblinking eyes as the magic pulsed around me. A whirlwind of dust, debris, and holy flame erupted around us, cutting us off from the others in the cavern. For a moment, I thought it would consume Ronan and me, burning us to ash instantly.

But there was no pain. In fact, it felt peaceful and almost comforting inside the swirling inferno. I stared down at Ronan, waiting for him to open his eyes. Slowly the cacophony around me began to cease. A gentle voice on the wind came to my ears, and I looked up, searching the flames for some hint of its source.

"A child of the Twilight calls upon me," the smooth female voice said. "It has been a long time since I answered their summons."

I glanced over my shoulder, my gaze falling upon a tall woman draped in sheer white fabric. She had dark skin and curling hair that spilled over her shoulders. Her golden eyes were soft and welcoming, glowing softly like the sun peeking over the horizon at dawn. In one hand, she held a long slender wand like a staff, the sharp point resting on the hard floor. She wore a soft, welcoming expression, but one eyebrow was lifted in curiosity. I knew who she was the moment I laid eyes on her.

"G-Goddess... of the Twilight," I muttered, bowing my head. "My lady... I c-can't believe it's y-you."

She stepped closer, the sheer white fabric sending off golden shimmers as it shifted. Kneeling beside me, she reached out, one large hand cupping my face. She was as big as Ronan, maybe bigger, and I couldn't help the fear welling up inside of me like I'd done something terribly wrong. No one had ever spoken of contacting the actual *gods* before.

"Still your mind, child," she cooed. "There's nothing to fear." She glanced down at Ronan, a small smile on her face. "You wish to save this man's life, and I have answered your call."

"R-Really?" I stuttered. "Is such a thing possible? When he... he's so... damaged."

She nodded. "It is. But only with my help. The magic your order does is simple, an innate talent that doesn't require my blessing. But with my help, so much more is possible."

I couldn't hide my look of surprise. What did she mean the clerics didn't have her blessing?

"The clerics of your world... they have fallen from the way of the Twilight," she said as if she could read my mind. "And have invented their own rules falsely in my name." Her expression shifted, a hint of sadness pulling at her delicate features. "There are few who walk the world that know the truth of my teachings, and even fewer who have any true power."

"The teachings... are wrong?"

She nodded. "Yes. The clerics have grown greedy and false, using their gifts only to gain dominion over others. They seek to live forever, either through their deeds or by magical means. They have lost the true meaning of the twilight."

"What... What is the true meaning?"

"Balance," she sighed. "The twilight marks the dawn and the dusk, the beginning and end of life. It is the moment where life and death converge in glorious splendor, the beauty of both evident for all to see." She placed a hand on my shoulder, leaning in close. "And you possess that gift, the power to give life and the power to take it away."

"You mean... the necromancy?" I asked, pulling away from her. "You think that's something I should *use*?"

"You saved your friends with it, did you not?"

"I... I don't..." I stuttered, shaking my head.

"There is a time for life and a time for death. Both are inevitable for everything that walks the world. Even me." She took a deep breath, her golden eyes searching mine. "And if you embrace that balance and walk the true path of the Twilight as my champion, I will bestow upon you my power."

"Will it be enough to save Ronan?" I asked, glancing down at him.

"It would be. But no matter your choice, I will grant this boon to you." She waved her hand over Ronan, the wound in his chest glowing a bright gold as it slowly knit itself back together. "The man you care for will live either way."

A wave of relief washed over me, tears forming in my eyes as emotions threatened to overwhelm me. I didn't understand who she was or why I cared for this strange man, but I couldn't help feeling a deep gratitude toward her. I stared as his chest rose, breath filling his body once more. He was going to be all right.

"What would you have me do as your champion?" I asked, willing to listen after such a generous gift.

"Fight to spread the true word of the Twilight across the land. The gods are not meant to be separated; we only represent a fraction of the cosmos you live in. Our words and deeds were not meant to be worshiped but to guide mankind to peace and prosperity. All are welcome, except those that would purposefully steal that peace away for selfish gain. Death is not the enemy, but tyranny and malice are."

I felt Ronan's chest slowly rise and fall under my hand, the purpose of my magic already complete. Thousands of questions were racing through my mind, and I could already feel the holy inferno around me fading.

"Reserve your answer for now," she said softly. Reaching out, she took my hand in hers. "When you are ready, I will be waiting."

Her form slowly started to fade as the conflagration around me lessened. With one last burst of white light, the cyclone broke, shattering into a million pieces as if made of glass instead of flame. At that exact moment, the Goddess of the Twilight vanished, her warm touch disappearing from my hand.

All that was left of her presence was a thin silver ring with an amber gem around my middle finger. It pulsed with a soft light, a pleasant warmth spreading through my hand.

So she was real, after all.

Eighteen: Dante

"Are you okay?" Kai asked, pulling his arm away from his eyes. "What happened?"

But I wasn't listening. I focused wholly on Ronan as I watched his chest slowly rise and fall. True to her word, he was alive once more. His eyes fluttered as he came to consciousness, turning his head to stare up at me.

"D-Dante?" he rasped, his voice weak.

"Just rest," I replied, stroking the side of his cheek. "You're going to be okay."

"By the gods..." Kai hissed behind me. "You... You brought him back to life? And his wounds... they're gone!" He reached down, grabbing me by the shoulder. "Can you help the others? The humans?"

I returned his gaze, slowly shaking my head. "No... this... this was a one-time thing. I'm not strong enough to help them too." I turned back to Ronan, savoring the feeling of the bond as it swelled between us once more, reassuring me that he was going to be all right. "We'll have to leave the others behind."

Kai clicked his tongue but didn't say a word. He knew as well as I that bringing someone back from such a state was a nearly unheard-of feat. The fact that it had happened even once was a miracle. I watched him stand in my periphery, heading back toward his hammer before going over to Torval. I kept my eyes fixed on Ronan, stroking his cheek or brushing away a dark stray hair. Having come so close to losing him, I was starting to realize how much he'd grown on me. For some werewolf asshole, he wasn't so bad.

"You... You saved me?"

I shook my head. "I tried to... but I wasn't strong enough."

"Then how am I still alive?"

"The Goddess of the Twilight saved you... as a gift to me."

Ronan rolled his eyes, groaning under his breath. "Stop it with this religious bullshit all the time. You and I both know the gods are just made up to men have an excuse to be terrible." He looked me dead in the eye. "The Clerics of the Twilight are the most guilty of that too, but I think you know that already."

My gut reaction was to shoot him down, to say something snide, and walk away. Instead, I took a deep breath and steadied myself.

"The goddess said the same thing," I murmured. "And... And I'm starting to think she was telling the truth."

Ronan's eyes widened, but he made no further comment. The look of surprise on his face told me all I needed to know. He never believed I'd change my thinking, and before that moment, I might have agreed with him. But between our group, the goddess, and the inconsistencies from Master Ryker, too many chips had been taken out of my spiritual armor. With every passing moment, I felt another crack form, exposing me to the truth of the world around me. Maybe... Maybe things were different than I'd been told. I wasn't sure if I was ready to believe it yet, but I could keep my eyes open and ask questions.

"Find a place to rest," I called out to the others. "We stay here until we're recovered enough to travel. The danger is behind us."

"What about the fallen?" Torval replied, his deep voice echoing in the chamber.

"We'll give them a proper burial before we leave."

There were grunts of approval as Kai and Torval turned away from the carnage before them. The sound of boots faded into the distance as they went to a far-off alcove, trying to find some semblance of peace and comfort as they rested. Ronan and I were left to fend for ourselves.

"Can... Can you help me to the water?" Ronan asked, not quite looking me in the eye.

He was massive, and I wasn't sure how much help I'd be.

"I'll try," I replied.

With some effort, I managed to get him to his feet. He grunted in pain over and over but didn't outwardly complain. I couldn't imagine a half-regrown torso was a comfortable feeling, but it was better than being dead. He'd get used to it.

With my arm around his waist, his bulky form leaning into me, we limped across the stone floor. His boots clanked against the stone, and I could still smell the sweat and blood coming off him in waves. I wasn't sure if he planned to wash or drink half the lake, but I hoped it was partially the former. His spicy man smell was much better than the metallic tang of blood and battle. I wanted him back to his former self.

And if I was being honest, I wanted a lot more than that. Having almost lost him, I realized how much I'd held myself back. Was it so wrong to go after the things I wanted? The goddess didn't seem to think so. And I felt this would probably be my last chance before we returned to the surface. If I returned to the temple, I'd never see Ronan again. But could I give up my place in the order? It might be true that the master clerics weren't telling us everything or that the goddess' teachings had become twisted over time. But that didn't necessarily mean I wanted to give up my life for some guy I'd just met. The pain of going to bed hungry every night was still fresh in my memory. At the temple, I had food, shelter, a station, and even a friend I cared for. Was Ronan worth leaving all that behind?

I didn't know the answer, but I wouldn't waste our limited private time anymore.

"Ronan?" I asked rather timidly.

"Yeah?"

"Can I... Can I talk to you?"

He glanced at me, raising an eyebrow. "You already are."

"No... I mean about what *happened*."

"Me dying or us fucking?"

I paused for a moment. "Both, I guess."

"Fire away," he grunted as I lowered him to the lake's edge. He lay flat on the floor, hanging his head over the water so he could drink. "I'm listening."

I sat down beside him, trying to get a better idea of what I wanted to say. I just let him drink for a long moment, helping him shift forward when he wanted to start scrubbing the blood off his arms and face. I took a deep breath to calm myself. It was now or never.

"The goddess helped me save you," I finally said.

"So I didn't make that up," he replied, looking up at me. "I thought it was just a dream."

"It wasn't a dream. She really came, the Goddess of the Twilight." I paused for a moment, wondering how much he remembered. "She... She told me a lot of things."

"Like what?"

"Like that, her teachings have been warped by the Clerics of the Twilight," I said, the floodgates bursting open. "That I've been lied to about her ways, that the magic I've done all my life wasn't a gift from her at all. She said the Masters of my order are stealing from people, bleeding them dry as they attempt to find a way to make themselves immortal." I looked up at Ronan, trying to fight back the tears in my eyes. "She saved you for me because she said I care about you. It was a gift to get me to consider being her personal champion."

"And what do you think?"

"I don't know if I have what it takes to be a champion of anyone, much less a goddess."

"No," Ronan replied. "That's not the part I was talking about."

My breath hitched in my throat. "I... I don't know what you mean."

He sighed. "It's no wonder the Masters find it so easy to lie to you," he said simply. "You can't even stop lying to yourself."

I furrowed my brows. "What do you m-"

"You know *exactly* what I mean," he snapped, pushing himself up from the water's edge. "I know you feel the bond between us too!

It's got nothing to do with your magic anymore, and it hasn't for a while. Five minutes ago, you were willing to summon powerful magic, sacrificing yourself to save me." He looked me dead in the eye, shimmers of gold around his pupils. "You're going to sit here and tell me it was for no reason? That you don't care for me even the slightest bit?"

I stared at him, my mouth hanging open as I tried to form a convincing lie that refused to take shape. He was right, of course. I knew full well a resurrection spell could kill me. I didn't even know if such magic was possible with or without the crystal shard. In a moment of desperation, I'd flung my well-being to the wind, willing to sacrifice it all just to save him.

So why was it so hard to admit it now?

"You want me," Ronan growled, reaching up and pulling me close to him, his meaty hand gripping the front of my robes. "And I want you. I didn't want to admit it to myself or anyone else, but... I *need* you."

His eyes were glowing once more, erupting into gold in the darkness. They were mesmerizing and beautiful, but they reminded me of the animal living within him. The beast that I'd been taught to fear my entire life.

"It... It's not safe."

"Not safe?" he snorted. "Nothing in this world is safe!" He pulled me closer, his face only inches from mine. "Tell me, what did I do to make you fear me so much? Or are your master's lies pulling you away from me?"

I swallowed hard. He was so close to me, enough to kiss me or tear my throat out. But even though he'd pulled me close, forcing me to be near him, his movements weren't those of aggression or anger. It was passion and confusion that spurred him forward. He wanted answers, and after everything we'd been through, I figured I could at least give him that.

"You... You were shifting after... after what we did," I finally managed to force out. "I thought... I thought you might kill me."

Ronan's jaw fell open. "Why *the fuck* would I do that?"

"I don't know," I said, shaking my head. I felt foolish to say it, but I had to tell him the truth. "I remember the fury you felt when you shifted in battle, the absolute *rage* toward those goblins. I thought... maybe I'd be next."

Ronan's grip on my robes loosened as he sat back on his heels. "You think I'm a monster still, don't you?"

"No! I don't..." I sighed heavily. "I don't know anything about this... this *thing* inside of you. I've been told my whole life that it's nothing more than a dangerous curse. That people like you slaughtered entire villages for fun, just to satiate your bloodlust. I don't think *you* would do that, but the beast?" I shrugged. "I just don't know."

His head nodded, eyes still cast down at the stone.

"Most of the world thinks the same as you," he replied at last, his voice cold and distant. "I've just grown used to it with time."

The melancholy seeping through his words brought me to my knees before him. I reached out, taking his vast calloused hands in mine.

"Will you tell me the truth then?" I asked, reaching out to stroke the side of his cheek. "The Twilight has kept me in limbo for so long." I leaned forward, my lips only inches from his. "Will you bring me into the light?"

"No," he replied, his golden eyes staring into mine. "But I can take you into the darkness. The place where people like me live their lives."

Nineteen: Ronan

Dante's eyes widened as he stared at me. I could see my words processing behind his gaze, my response not quite what he'd expected. But that wasn't what he asked for. He wanted to know the truth, the reality behind my situation, and the life I had to lead in order to survive in Eadronem. I wasn't going to sugarcoat it for him.

"Tell me," he said at last with a slight nod. "Tell me everything about your life."

His words rang with candor, his earnestness palpable. I felt myself take a deep breath, a dull ache spreading through my chest from where the fatal wound had been only moments before. I'd never told anyone about my life or the Brotherhood, but Dante was going to learn it all. For years I'd been avoiding showing my true self to anyone. And although I knew a cleric was probably the last person I should open up to, I couldn't help but trust Dante. He'd saved my life, and I'd saved his. If that didn't earn a person's trust, I didn't know what would.

"I was bitten when I was sixteen," I sighed. "It was my first trip to the autumnal festival in Jyra with my family. We stopped to camp on the road one night out from the city. I awoke to the sounds of my mother and father fighting to protect me and my younger sister, but they were no match." I paused for a moment, forcing back the flood of memories. "We ran into the woods, trying to hide from the monsters pursuing us, the sounds of our parent's screams filling our ears. We found a tree to hide in, but my sister wouldn't stop crying. I tried to save her when the beasts ripped us out of the branches, but they silenced her forever before I could do anything."

Dante's hand was on his lips, his eyes wide.

"I don't know why they let me live," I continued. "Maybe they were already satiated from feasting on my family and our wares. For whatever reason, they left me in those woods, bleeding from a large bite wound across my shoulder." I reached up instinctively, rubbing the wound that had long healed into nothing but tiny scars. "And by some miracle... or curse, I lived. Most people die after being bitten. The disease is too strong and destroys their bodies. But I survived, somehow. I don't really understand why, but when I finally came a couple of days later, I was completely healed. Not only that, I felt strong, so much more than before. With nothing of my family left but bones picked clean by scavengers, I turned toward town. My only saving grace was that the Brotherhood found me before my first full moon."

"That... that's horrible," Dante said, his hand still covering his lips. "Why did they do that to your family?"

"They were feral, slaves to the beast that lived inside them," I nodded. "The Brotherhood killed their roving band after I told them my story. My family was avenged, just not by me like I'd hoped."

"What... What is the Brotherhood?"

I sighed heavily. "The Brotherhood is a secret band of shifters that operate out of sight in all the major cities in Eadronem. They take in people like me and ensure we control ourselves. And those that lose control... well, they get rid of them. Permanently."

"That's terrifying."

I shrugged. "It's the only thing keeping the people of Eadronem safe from what happened to me. I wouldn't wish that night on anyone."

Dante looked as if he regretted everything he'd ever said to me. His features were twisted into a deep guilt that rolled off him in waves. But for me, it was just a regular thing. People were scared of werewolves for good reasons. There were still those wandering through the world wishing to harm anything that crossed their path should the mood strike them. However, that was no different from anyone else. The clerics were known to be cruel, the military even more so. But nobody universally feared them like they did my kind or those like Kai and Torval. It was a strange irony that the world seemed to ignore.

"I... I shouldn't have said..." Dante began.

"It's fine," I replied, waving him off. "Really. You're not the only one."

"That doesn't make it better."

"No, I guess not," I sighed. "And I should apologize to you too. I hated you from the start for just being a cleric. That wasn't fair."

"I was a dick..."

"And I wasn't?"

We both laughed, our voices echoing over the still water as the tension finally broke between us. It was a strange moment of peace but one I relished. It had been a long time since I felt so comfortable in another's company. We sat at the edge of the lake, side by side, just enjoying a moment of calm together.

"Dante?" I said, at last, staring out over the lake.

"Yeah?"

"Will you spend one last night with me?"

I saw him turn toward me in my periphery, a look of confusion on his face.

"You and I both know this can't last," I sighed. "The moment we set foot outside this mine, we'll be torn apart. You can't go with me into the world, and I can't go with you to the temple." I reached out, placing a hand on his thigh and squeezing it gently. "But we can share one last moment, can't we?"

Dante nodded slowly, his eyes catching the crystalline light more than usual. "Y-Yeah. I didn't want to believe it, but I know you're right." He leaned in close, placing a soft kiss on my lips. "One last night."

I slipped my hand around the back of Dante's neck, pulling him against me once more. Our lips met his parting quickly to let my tongue inside. His scent filled my lungs, his taste in my mouth simultaneously filling me with joy and dread. Come this time tomorrow; he'd be gone, his delicate form never held in my hands again. I squeezed him tighter, pressing his body against my chest. If this would be my last night with him, I would commit every inch of him to memory.

My fingers worked their way between the folds of his robes until I found skin. I knew my hands were rough, and I was careful not to mar his beautiful form. He was warm and soft, the perfect antithesis of myself. I pulled away from his lips, working my own across his jaw and neck, taking small nibbles at his ear as I worked my way down. Little moans reverberated in his throat, making my cock throb against the leather of my pants. But my dick would have to wait. Tonight was all about the man in front of me.

"Hold on," he said, pulling away from me. "Let's get you cleaned up first."

"Right," I nodded, remembering I was still covered in my own blood. "Sorry."

Dante shook his head with a smile, helping me with the straps of my armor. It took a few minutes to get through all of them; the heat between us put on pause for only a moment. Once my leather armor was pushed off to the side, he helped me with my clothing, my thick cock bouncing free as the leather trousers were removed. Dante gave it a soft squeeze before pointing me toward the water. Doing as he commanded, I swung my legs over the edge of the lake. A sharp breath hissed through my teeth as the freezing cold water surrounded me. The shock of the cold made me want to abandon it altogether, but I wasn't ready to give up my night with Dante for a minute or two of discomfort.

"Wait," he said, tapping me on the shoulder. "I'll come in with you."

He took a step back, reaching down to pull at the clasp of his robes. With a single click, they fell to the ground, pooling around his feet. Slowly he unfastened each button of his shirt, tossing it aside as he pulled it off. His trousers followed suit a moment later, left in the pile of fabric beside my armor. He took a step back, giving me a moment to drink him in. My eyes caressed his body, taking in every subtle curve and edge that made him so beautiful. His cock, like my own, was rock hard, a single drop of glistening precum gathering at its tip. I reached out and pulled him close, licking the sweet nectar and letting his taste bloom across my tongue.

"You are so beautiful," I said. "And you taste incredible."

I reached out again to pull him close, but he batted my hands away.

"We wash first," he chuckled, pointing me back toward the water. Sitting down beside me, he slipped his legs into the lake. "Oh fuck!" he hissed, locking up his muscles. "That's freezing!"

"Let's make it quick then," I replied, pushing myself up and off the edge.

The water was too dark to tell how deep it was, but I was still surprised when my head slipped under the surface, my feet finding no purchase below me. Thankfully I kept one hand on the sheer underwater cliff that comprised the shore. I flexed my arm, pulling myself back to the surface just in time to see Dante slip in after me, but he wasn't holding onto anything.

My hand plunged beneath the surface, grabbing his arm and yanking him back up before he could go too far. His head broke through a second later as he gasped for air. Apparently, he'd expected a solid surface to stand on as well.

"Come on," I laughed, nudging him toward the edge. "Wash fast and get back up there before you freeze to death."

He nodded, already shivering as he quickly scrubbed himself with his bare hands. It wasn't a proper bath, but it would be enough to get the grime and blood off of us both. I followed suit, and within a matter of moments, we'd both heaved our naked bodies back up onto the stone. The air around us seemed even colder than before. Dante retrieved his cloak, waving me over to a small alcove where we could have some privacy. The cold shock had killed both of our erections, but as Dante settled between my legs, leaning back against my chest, I felt my cock stir again.

I wrapped the cloak around my shoulders, reclining against the stone with my arms crossed over Dante's chest. My knees were pulled up on either side of him, forming a kind of cocoon with his body pressed up against me. We were both chattering, our bodies still in shock.

"Maybe this will help," Dante said, rubbing his hands together.

With a whisper of an incantation under his breath, his hands suddenly glowed with a soft amber light, like the flickering of a candle. He placed one on my chest and the other on his own. The moment he touched my skin, I felt a wave of warmth flood my body, the shivers driven away in an instant. I wasn't sure if it was the heat or his touch that got me going again, but I was extremely aware of my cock wedged into the small of his back, its pulsing heat against his skin.

"This... isn't quite comfortable," he said, pulling his hand away.

"Sorry..." I reached down and tried to adjust myself to get my dick out of the way. "I didn't mean for it to-"

My words were cut off as Dante turned around, wrapping his legs around my waist so that he was facing me, and slowly lowered himself back down. I felt his erection throb as it slid down my chest, leaving a trail of precum in its wake. He came to rest on my hips, his legs pulling him against me with my rod pressed firmly between his butt cheeks. I couldn't help but let out a small moan as he shifted, trying to get more comfortable. The friction was already driving me crazy.

"That's better," he said, wrapping his arms around my neck. A mischievous smirk played across his lips. "Now I can see you better." He leaned in close, his lips brushing against mine. "And kiss you."

Before I could even form a thought, his lips were pressed to mine, his tongue swirling around my own. I relaxed, letting him take the reigns. There was so much I wanted to say to him, to explain if I could. But I knew none of it would create a future where we could both be together. Instead, I gave into the moment, letting it consume me. The memories would be all I had to comfort me once the mission was over.

"Stop thinking," Dante said, tearing his lips away from me. "And just touch me."

I nodded, acquiescing to the hunger in his voice. A pulse of adrenaline shot through my system, and I felt my eyes throb, indicating that they'd just shifted completely to gold. Dante smiled and leaned in once more, his kisses deeper and more passionate.

My fingers trailed across his back, outlining the curves of his shoulder blades before diving further down. His skin was so soft, and his scent was overpowering. I breathed him in deeply, drinking in every bit of him. He moaned into my mouth as my hands found his ass, gripping both cheeks and squeezing. My cock pulsed against his entrance, my knot already forming as my excitement mounted. I wanted to fuck him... badly. But he was only human and much smaller than me. It might not be the greatest idea.

As if reading my mind, Dante reached back and began to pump my cock between his cheeks. Using my precum as lube, he stroked up and down, rocking his hips in time with his hand. Electricity shot up my spine, my balls tensing with each passing movement. He was driving me crazy. Leaning against me and popping his butt out, he grabbed my rod and pushed the crown against his hole. A low growl echoed through my chest, the slow circles he was making against the head of my cock diminishing my willpower with every passing moment.

"You d-don't have to do that," I heaved, the sensation of his hole pressing against my cock almost too much to bear. "I... I don't w-want to hurt you."

Dante glared at me, his hand behind his back, still stroking my shaft between his cheeks. "I want you," he said with a determined expression. "*All* of you."

"Fuck..." I groaned, digging my fingers into his hips. "I love that look in your eyes."

"Go slow," he moaned, leaning back against my throbbing cock. "But don't stop."

"Yes, sir."

It was a good thing his ass was slick with precum because he was tight. It took a few tries to get his hole to stretch out, each attempt allowing a little bit more of me in. I did everything I could to resist bucking forward, allowing him to take me at his own pace. After a moment or two, a sharp gasp passed between his lips as the head of my cock slipped past his ring. He leaned forward, breathing heavily as he rested his head on my shoulder.

"Fuck..." he gasped. "You're... so big..."

"Take your time," I replied, holding him tightly.

He relaxed into me further, letting gravity take over. I ran my hands over his body, planting kisses along his neck and shoulder as his hole slowly widened to accommodate my girth. With each passing moment, he slipped a little further down my cock, the achingly slow pace driving me wild. I felt every inch of him gripping me, the friction making my entire body break out in goose flesh. Eventually, he came to rest at the top of my half-formed knot.

"You don't have to go any further," I whispered into his ear, feeling him tremble in my grip.

"I... I want it."

His words touched some deep animalistic place inside me, a deep purr rising from the core of my chest. I merely nodded, letting him go so he could set the pace. I tried to reach down to give his cock some attention too, but he batted me away. Instead, he leaned back, lifting himself until my cock nearly came free. Then, with agonizing slowness, he began to slide back down, his hole swallowing my cock nearly to the hilt.

"Fuck," he moaned, his head tilted back toward the ceiling. "You feel so good... and thick...."

"You feel good, too," I replied, my hands gripping his hips as he slid upwards once more. "Fuck you're so tight."

Words were replaced with moans as Dante continued to work his hole up and down my shaft, savoring every last inch of my body. I leaned back, my hands resting on his hips as he used my body for his pleasure. I was happy to do it, to give him everything he wanted. Each stroke was a lesson in torture, but I held myself back. He wasn't going to get my load until he begged for it.

"You like that big cock?" I asked, feeling his pace start to quicken. "Bet I'm touching you in places you didn't even know were possible."

"Fuck yes," Dante moaned, arching his back. "I've never... felt anything like this before."

"Good boy," I growled, letting the sound reverberate through my entire body.

Dante pushed back even harder, his hole stretching against my knot. The first couple of bounces didn't get very far, but after a minute or so, I could feel him opening up to me. Even the most talented courtesans couldn't take all of me. Was this inexperienced cleric going to show them all up? The combination of his tenacity and the friction between us was summoning up the wolf inside of me. I felt my fingers extend, claws pressing against Dante's smooth flesh. Fangs elongated from my jaw as fur erupted across my body. My cock swelled even further, making him cry out in ecstasy as it pulsed inside him. He was leaking an alarming amount of precum across my belly, his crown sliding over my skin.

"Fuck," Dante moaned, leaning back further. "Fuck I'm getting close. But... I need *more*."

That last word nearly put me over the edge. Digging my fingers into his hips, I held him in place, my knot pressed against his hole. I felt it slip nearly halfway in, the thickest point of my cock nearly past his ring. He pushed harder, his hole stretching to its limits.

Then, with a small pop, I felt my knot slip inside, my first time ever fully inside another man. The sensation was almost too much to describe, filling my body with world-shifting tingles from head to toe.

Dante seemed to be getting even more from it as he collapsed against me, breathing heavily, constantly moaning into my neck.

"Fuck," I whispered, kissing his neck. "I can't believe you did it."

"I'm so close," he shuddered, his body fully resting on top of me. "But I feel like pudding."

"You've done the hard part," I replied, nipping at his ear. "I'll take it from here."

Holding him tightly against me, I began to rock my hips back and forth, my knot pulling at his ring from the inside. He made the most pitiful noises into my neck, each one turning me on more and more.

"You okay?" I asked.

"Don't stop," he whispered. "By the gods... *don't stop.*"

And I did what I was told.

Keeping the same pace, I continued to plunge my throbbing werewolf cock deeper and deeper into his tunnel, the friction growing more and more as my knot engorged. I was getting close, and judging by the shuddering moans against my neck, Dante was too.

"Fuck... Fuck I'm close," I gasped, my strokes growing more erratic.

"Me too..."

I felt my abs tense as my balls drew up. I only had a few seconds left.

"Fuck... I'm gonna..."

But Dante beat me to it. He arched his back, crying out toward the ceiling as warm ropes of sticky cum splashed across my chest, his cock throbbing with each new release. At the same moment, I felt my own orgasm reach its peak, my entire body tensing up as I filled his hole. I came again and again, each pulse filling his tunnel with my seed. His moans doubled as my knot pulsed with each shot, milking even more cum out of his already spent body.

Dante collapsed back against me, my knot still lodged firmly in his ass. A wave of warmth and peace washed over me as we lay there, both of us heaving from the intensity of our orgasms. My vision was blurred, the room around me darker than I remembered as stars popped into existence at my periphery. In all my life, I'd never had someone do what Dante did, taking all of me down to the hilt. Knotting him was the most incredible feeling in the entire world, and I wanted to do it again and again.

There was just one problem.

"Uh... Dante?"

"Yeah," he replied breathlessly.

"I think... uh... we're kinda stuck together for a little while."

He leaned back, wincing as my still rock-hard cock shifted inside him. "What do you mean?"

"You took all of it," I replied. "That knot isn't going down for a while."

He shifted, trying to prove me wrong by lifting himself off it. But he didn't get anywhere. While he was riding me, I'd shifted; further, the knot growing inside him. It wasn't coming out until it was ready. He stared down at me, a horrified look on his face as the truth settled in.

"It's okay," I said before he could lose his mind. "We'll just sleep here. Together. Nobody will know."

"Are... Are you sure?" He tried to glance back at the knot tying us together. "It's not gonna be like that forever?"

"I'm sure," I chuckled. Or at least I was fairly sure. The other werewolves had talked about it from time to time, but I wasn't going to let him know my uncertainty. "Everything will be fine."

"I... I guess I did kinda want to sleep in your arms," he replied, his cheeks flushing in embarrassment. "Stupid, huh?"

"No." I pulled him close, squeezing him against my chest. With my free hand, I threw the cloak around us to shield us from the cold of the cavern. "I wouldn't have it any other way."

Twenty: Dante

Sleeping with a werewolf knot shoved up my ass shouldn't have been easy. But somehow, after our tandem orgasms, I found it simple to fall asleep cradled in Ronan's arms. His warmth surrounded me, filling me with a sense of peace and safety that I realized I'd never felt before. Being in his arms felt right, like I belonged there, even though I knew the morning would pull us apart. We'd head back to our old lives like nothing had changed. I didn't know about him, but I was fairly certain my life would never be the same. Between our night together and my interaction with the Goddess of the Twilight, there was no going back to my old ways.

It felt as if all of Eadronem had changed. But the truth was, nothing had changed. Just me.

My sleep was punctuated by dreams about Ronan and what our lives could be if we ran off together. I dreamed of faraway adventures, just the two of us traveling across the world on horseback or with a small cart of our own. We'd move from town to town, taking jobs that suited our own skills. Ronan would fight off the monsters causing issues with the villagers while I tended to their wounds and diseases. Everyone loved us, and nobody cared about our pasts or what we were. Instead, they saw us for who we were and praised us for our deeds. Nights would find him and myself near a campfire on the road, our bodies intertwined in the flickering light. Each moment passing between us filled with ecstasy.

Then as all dreams eventually do, they came to an end, forcing me out of the bliss I longed to stay in forever. I fought against it, of course, snuggling further into Rona's chest and forcing my eyes closed. I wanted to go back... *needed* it to be true once more. But no matter how hard I struggled, I remained awake. Instead, I focused on the soft rhythm of his breathing, enjoying the last moments with him that I could.

Sometime during the night, his knot had gone down, and he pulled out of me. I could still feel the dull ache in my ass, but I was glad for it. At least for a couple of days, I'd have something to remember him by. He was already hard again in his sleep, his thick cock pulsing against my ass. I had half a mind to push it back in, to ride his knot again, so we had no choice but to leave. But I knew no matter how much I tried to put it off; it would never last. There was nothing to eat in the cavern, and our supplies were already running dangerously low. Not to mention there was probably the remainder of a pissed-off goblin tribe still searching for us. It would just be a matter of time before they found us and overwhelmed our diminished party. With two people down, we didn't stand a chance.

That thought led me to another. The humans... they still needed to be buried. I'd nearly forgotten about them in my passion for Ronan. But it was my duty as the cleric to see that they were laid to rest in the most agreeable way possible. With the cavern made entirely of stone, burying them in soil wouldn't be an option. However, the lake provided an opportunity to give them a sailor's burial. It wasn't much, but we couldn't risk taking them back to the surface and slowing our progress. Besides, one of them was far too damaged to move about, her body crushed under the worm.

I still couldn't figure out why Master Ryker had told me they were monsters. It was possible there had been some last-minute changes he didn't know about, but I'd never known him to make a mistake like that before. He was well known among the temple as the most informed and ambitious cleric. No, I had a feeling he labeled them monsters because they were from beyond the borders of Eadronem. They brought knowledge and ideas with them that could harm the teachings of the temple and possibly the state. If there was one thing the Clerics of the Twilight didn't stand for, it was harm to the state.

I had to get to the bottom of things as soon as I got back. It would take no small amount of tact to sift through the temple's lies and figure out their true intentions, but I figured it could be done within a couple of years. Calder would help me too; he loved doing things he wasn't supposed to. This would be a well-received gift in his eyes. Then, once I'd found out the truth, I would present my decision to the Goddess herself. A part of me wanted to answer her now, but I still held my allegiance to the temple. After all, they'd taken me off the streets, fed me, given me a home, and practically guaranteed me a comfortable life for as long as I lived. That had to count for something. I couldn't just abandon them without investigating. I knew they weren't without fault, but the Goddess made it sound like the clerics were downright evil, and I wasn't willing to accept that at just her word.

Ronan stirred below me as I leaned my head back against his chest. His large hands reached up, both of them crossing over my back and pulling me in tighter. He gave a drowsy snort, his hips rocking upward as he ground his hard cock against my ass reflexively. The sensation made me shudder, goose flesh erupting across my body. My erection was already blissfully pressed against his torso, the friction causing a slow ooze of precum from my cock.

"Careful there," I whispered, kissing his neck. "I'm not sure we have time to repeat that again."

"Wha-?" he mumbled, opening one bleary eye. "Oh... right. Sorry."

He started to move away, but I tightened my grip around his neck.

"Just... just let me enjoy it for a few more minutes."

He nodded, knowing full well that this would be our last chance to be close like this.

"Okay."

I wasn't sure how long I laid there like that, just wrapped up in his arms. The warmth made me drowsy again, even though I knew it wouldn't be enough to put me back to sleep. For a moment longer, I allowed myself to dream. But it came to an end all too quickly as we heard the others rustling in a nearby alcove. A streak of embarrassment raced through my body as I sat up. If I could hear the simple shifting of their clothing and armor, they certainly heard what Ronan and I had done the night before.

"Don't worry," Ronan whispered in my ear as if he could read my thoughts. "They won't say anything."

I wasn't convinced. "How do you know?"

"People like us... we look out for one another." He placed a small kiss on my cheek. "They know how... *odd* our pairing is. It'll just be seen as a passing fancy. We... We all know it can't be any more than that."

Those last few words were cold and empty, the light in Ronan's eyes growing dark. The tone of his voice nearly broke my heart, although I didn't really understand why. I knew in my mind that what he said was true, but my heart... well, it wasn't quite ready to believe it just yet.

I nodded anyway, trying not to let the chill affect me too much. "Right." Leaning forward, I gave him one last soft kiss on the lips. "I guess we should get dressed."

"Yeah..." he sighed. "I guess we should.

***

A few hours later found us entering the mines once more, leaving the crystalline caves and the underground lake behind us for good. Our human companions had been laid to rest in the lake as planned, where they sunk into the dark depths, never to be seen again. Our only consolation was that they were together, although even that seemed like a poor prize for people who would never see the light of day again.

The way back had been easier, our packs lighter and the path familiar. But the air around us was heavy. Torval and Kai were silent while Ronan and I walked side by side. Every now and then, our hands would touch, the temptation to intertwine our fingers so strong that we had to force ourselves further apart. It was torture.

As we made our way back through the mines, I found myself counting down the minutes until we'd part ways forever. I'd grown fond of Torval and Kai, their protection having saved my life and their words providing companionship along the way. They weren't the monsters I'd been expecting. Instead, they were just people who happened not to be human. That was all. Ronan, of course, was no different. If there was one thing I'd be certain never to do again, it was judge people for the way they looked instead of the quality of their character. Looking back at my life, I realized I had a lot to make up for and even more people to tell off once I got back to the temple. That included Master Ryker, although I wasn't yet sure how I'd do it.

And, of course, I was dreading the moment I'd have to say goodbye to Ronan as well. It was a chill that settled in my chest, an unnamed anxiety that kept my breaths short and my muscles tight. With each passing step, I felt the distance between us grow. He was settling back into his old stony self while I gritted my teeth, trying to seem much tougher than I was. What had taken us days to overcome was gone in a matter of hours.

We passed by the rotting corpses of the goblins, the familiar path slipping away much faster than anticipated. Soon we could all make out the faintest hint of daylight in the distance. It should have filled me with excitement, but all I felt was dread. Kai and Torval pulled ahead of us, both eager to be out of the mines for good. I couldn't blame them.

They broke through into the bright sunlight, but I stayed behind, hanging back some ten feet into the tunnel. Leaning back against the wall, I tilted my head toward the ceiling, trying to force in a few deep breaths before I had to go back to my own world. Ronan stepped up in front of me, his fingers lightly tracing my waist.

"Are you all right?" he asked.

"I... I want to be," I replied. "But I'm not."

"I understand."

It was a simple answer, but the only one that made any sense. Both of us knew that no amount of words could change what was about to happen. I cursed myself for feeling things so deeply, for caring about him so much, even though I had only just met him a few days before.

Why had he gotten under my skin so much? Did he feel the same about me? Even if he did, it didn't matter. I was going back to the temple.

"I wish..." I began.

"Me too," he nodded, leaning forward. "Just promise me one thing, okay?'

"What's that?" I asked, wrapping my arms around his waist as his face inched closer to mine.

"Take care of yourself."

His lips were so close.

"Only... Only if you do the same."

"I promise."

I leaned into him, pressing his lips against my own. For a long moment, I let the heat pass between us, his tongue swirling around my own one last time. Even when he finally pulled away, I could still taste him on my lips.

"I'll do my best," I replied breathlessly.

"Good boy." Ronan placed a hand on my shoulder, turning me toward the mouth of the mine. "Go on. I'll be right behind you."

I nodded silently, unable to speak without my voice breaking. There were tears forming at the corners of my eyes, frustrating me to no end. I didn't want to cry, not in front of him. Things were hard enough already without having to deal with my emotional outbursts. In a few days time, I'd be fine, settling back into life at the temple once more. Although I had a feeling my dreams were never going to be the same again.

As I stepped out into the sunlight, I held up my arm to shield my eyes. A few cries echoed across the clearing that I couldn't make out. I figured it was the guard welcoming us back from the mines, surprised that we survived. However, as my eyes adjusted, I realized the shouts came from Kai and Torval as they were wrestled to the ground by several guards. Torval's staff had been broken, and Kai's hammer lay some distance away, lodged in the breastplate of what I assumed was a now-dead guard.

"What are you doing?" I called out. "What's the meaning of this?"

Nobody answered me. Spinning on my heel, I turned to warn Ronan about the ambush, but he was already barreling past me, his sword drawn.

"No!" I cried, my fingers grazing his back as I tried to reach for him. "Don't attack them!"

To my surprise, he stopped. His chest was heaving, his knuckles white, where he clutched the sword in his hand. He glanced back at me, his eyes golden with fury.

"I'll take care of this," I said. "Trust me."

Ronan took one last deep breath and threw his sword to the ground. Guards swarmed him the second it left his hand, allowing them to place manacles on his wrists and ankles.

"Captain!" I cried out, seeing the small fat man approaching. "What is the meaning of this? You would arrest your own saviors?"

"Orders from the top," he said coolly. "They are to be arrested on sight."

"These people saved my life! Protected me from untold dangers in those mines!" I shouted back at him.

He wasn't phased. "These *monsters* have broken the law," he replied. "And this one is a werewolf." He jabbed the butt of his dagger into Ronan's ribs. "That alone is enough to have him executed."

"They are nothing but dutiful citizens of Eadronem! Let them go!"

The captain stepped close, his stinking breath hot on my face. "You best watch yourself, young *acolyte*. Protecting monsters like these is seen as treason in the eyes of the state." He leaned back, pointing toward the end of the street. "Besides, *his* authority outweighs yours."

I followed his finger down the cobblestone road to a figure that stood some thirty feet away, shaded under a cloth awning near the garrison. It was Master Ryker, and he didn't look pleased.

Twenty-One: Dante

"Master Ryker!" I called, jogging up in front of him and his apprentice. "You have to let these people go. They saved my life in the mines! They deserve their pay and their freedom."

Ryker didn't turn toward me or even flick his gaze in my direction. Instead, he looked back out toward the captain of the guard.

"Take them to my ship," he commanded. "Make sure they are secure." He eyed Ronan suspiciously. "Especially the mongrel."

"Master Ryker, you have to stop thi—"

"If you do not cease this ill-placed pity, you will forfeit your promotion to full Cleric."

My mouth snapped shut immediately, my old habits of submission coming back to me. Ryker's tone was unlike anything I'd ever heard before. He always seemed so cool and calm, but something about my words had gotten under his skin.

"Not only are you late from your mission, but your behavior towards these *beasts* embarrasses the entire order," he spat. "You will not speak another word until we're back at the temple. Is that clear?"

I merely nodded, knowing not to test him further.

With a huffy nod, Ryker stormed down the street, his apprentice scrambling to keep up. I stood in place, my heart racing a mile a minute. My thoughts were so jumbled that I didn't know what to do. Defying Ryker would mean sacrificing my promotion, which I needed to get to the bottom of what was going on in the temple. I couldn't test the Goddess' claims if I wasn't allowed to get close to anyone in the temple. Not only that but defending my companions was considered treason, especially with a master giving the orders. If I tried to stop the guard, I'd be arrested, possibly even killed.

I didn't have a choice but to stand there as the guards slowly filed past me, dragging the prisoners through Terrastera toward the sky port and Ryker's airship. Kai and Torval looked at me, their eyes begging for help as they passed by. Ronan came up behind them, fighting every step of the way. He turned to me, his golden eyes blazing.

"Help us!" he yelled, trying to get closer to me.

I didn't move.

"HELP US!"

Tears threatened my cheeks, and I turned my gaze down toward the cobblestones. Ronan's struggling suddenly stopped, his breath ragged.

"Why... Why won't you stand up for us?"

My heart was beating so fast, but I knew better than to respond with the captain standing right there.

"You... You traitor..." Ronan whispered.

My gaze flicked up to his, the hurt and betrayal on his face breaking my heart in an instant. I watched as all the fight went out of him, his body slumping forward against the guards. They tore at him, dragging him across the stones and up the road. He was so defeated the powerful man I knew reduced to nothing but a mere shadow of his former self. And all of that because of me.

The captain beside me merely grinned and followed after his guards, leaving me standing there in the middle of the street with tears running down my cheeks. Ronan was right. I'd betrayed them all.

***

"Welcome back!" Calder cried, leaping up from his bed the moment I entered the room. "You did it! You're going to be a full Cleric now! Ryker's already announced it to the entire temple! Congratulations!"

"Thanks..." was all I could mutter in response.

I crossed the room and collapsed on my bed face first, my mind still reeling from the ride back to Aratis. After Ryker had called me to his cabin and dressed me down for fifteen minutes, telling me how stupid I was and ill-fit for the job, he offered me the promotion to Cleric as a 'keep your mouth shut' gift. He didn't want anyone to know what had happened to the people who cleared out the mines. Instead, he had already begun circulating a story that the Tide Fighters had done it themselves, the state's military coming to the aid of the common man. Nobody wanted to hear about the *monsters* that saved the people of Terrastera from untold dangers, and no noble wanted to be indebted to people such as them anyway. It was a perfect cover-up story to make it look like the state had been the hero all along, just like they wanted everyone to believe.

And me... well, I was supposed to keep quiet for all eternity as I enjoyed the spoils that came along with being an official Cleric of the Twilight. I knew the promotion was part bribe and part test. Ryker was seeing if I had what it took to keep my adventures to myself and let his lies spread through Terrastera and the temple. If I didn't do as he said, there was no doubt in my mind that I could wind up missing, a new lie percolating through the streets that I'd run away of my own accord or abandoned the temple. But the truth was much more terrifying than that. After everything I'd experienced in the last two hours, I had no doubt in my mind that the Goddess' claims had some validity. Now I just needed to figure out how deep they went.

"Just *thanks*?" Calder asked, plopping down on the bed next to me. "Aren't you excited? Getting to move up from Acolyte is a big deal! Especially for people our age! Most don't make it until they're well into their thirties!"

"Yeah, it's okay," I replied.

"Dante," he said, his hand resting on my shoulder. "What's going on?"

I glanced up at him, the joyful look in his eyes replaced by worry. He knew something was going on, and I knew I wasn't doing a good job of hiding it. After my meeting with the Goddess, I decided he would be the person I'd go to for help, the acolyte I'd choose as my apprentice. It was faster than I expected, but everything had gotten so topsy-turvy in the blink of an eye.

But none of that mattered. Ronan and his companions were imprisoned in the temple dungeons below our feet. They had maybe two days tops before they were executed that I was sure of. But with Calder's help, I might be able to find a way to stay their punishment, giving me time to find a way to set them free.

"Calder," I said, staring him dead in the eye. "I need you to be my acolyte."

His mouth fell open. "I... I accept," he smiled. There was a look of pure joy on his face like I knew there would be. He'd wanted to get out of the temple for years. "Of course, I'll be your apprentice."

"Good," I nodded. "Now I need you to help me save the people that protected me through the mines."

"I thought... Ryker said they were Tide Fighters. What do they need our help with?"

"They weren't Tide Fighters. They were people of monstrous origin; an orc, a Draak, and a werewolf. There were two humans as well from beyond the borders of Eadronem... but they didn't make it."

"Beyond the borders of Eadronem?" he scoffed. "That's impossible!"

"Many things we've been taught are impossible are, in fact, possible. Not to mention the mound of lies this entire temple is built upon."

Calder stared for a long moment. "I... I like what you're saying," he said at last. "Keep going."

"Well, first off, I had a visit from the Goddess of the Twilight."

"Shut the fuck up."

"It's true," I replied, unable to stop the small smirk at his reaction. "And she told me about a lot of things going on here that seem to be not only untrue but in purposeful opposition to her teachings." I leaned in close. "She thinks the Masters are trying to discover the secret to immortality, and she wants me to stop it."

"That's a big accusation."

"I know. That's why I wanted to try to gather some proof. But before we do that, I need to save my... my *friends* before the temple kills them."

He nodded. "Okay. How do we do that?"

"I'm not sure," I said, shaking my head. "Maybe we need to confront Ryker. Or one of the other Masters. Either way, we need to stop them from being executed because I know that's what's going to happen. If there's one thing the temple is known for, it's not putting up with people who would make it look bad."

"I know they protected you," Calder said slowly. "But sticking your neck out for them might cost you your life. Not to mention your station in the temple." He paused. "You... You know that, right?"

"I know," I nodded. "But it's worth it."

"Why?"

"It's... It's the right thing to do."

"Don't give me that bullshit," he scoffed. "Nobody does that shit in this world. Things are too hard to do the *right thing* all the time. What's the real reason?"

I hesitated for a long moment, wondering if I should tell him the truth. He stared at me, his eyes unblinking as he read my every move. I heaved a deep sigh, realizing that if I wanted Calder's help, he'd have to know everything.

"I... I fell in love."

His eyebrows shot up.

"With a werewolf."

His hand went to his mouth. "Oh... my... gods..."

"It's... It's not a big deal."

"Not a big deal!" he cried, throwing his hands up. "Not a big deal!"

"Keep your voice down!"

Calder slid closer to me, his shoulder pressed up against mine. "I'll be quiet only if you tell me absolutely everything that happened between you two. There's a lot of missing context here. And if you leave out even *one* juicy detail, I swear I will turn you into the Council of Masters in seconds flat. Deal?"

I sighed, knowing I had no other choice. "Deal..."

"Good." He snaked an arm around my shoulder. "Tell me how it all started."

"At the mines, obviously," I replied. "I thought he was such an asshole, to begin with."

"Oooh," Calder cooed. "I like this already."

"Sometimes I despise you. You know that?"

"That's obviously untrue," he said, waving me off. "Now continue."

I took a deep breath. It was going to be a long night.

Twenty-Two: Dante

Calder and I spent the majority of the night conversing after I'd finished my story. The early gray of dawn was grasping as the sky when we finally came to the end of our conversation. A cold breeze flowed through the open window, our candles flickering as they reached the ends of their wicks. In a few hours, our entire relationship had changed. Before, we'd just been friends, but now... now we were co-conspirators against the temple. At least, that's how they'd see it if anyone found out.

"It's just... hard to believe all this happened," Calder said. "I believe you, don't get me wrong. But it's a lot to take in." He glanced up at me, running his fingers through his hair with a sigh. "I know I'm not the paragon of acolytes in this temple, but I didn't think they were straight-up evil."

'That feels like a strong word," I replied. "I think some of them, especially Master Ryker, is up to something he shouldn't be. I don't know what it is, but at the very least, I'm concerned about his indifference to sending innocent people to prison."

"The orc and the Draak, I can understand," Calder nodded. "*Unfortunately,* he's in the right about the werewolf." He held up his hands before I could retort. "I'm not saying it's right! I'm just saying that it is the law. They aren't seen as people in the eyes of the state."

"Then the state is wrong too."

Calder stared at me, his jaw hanging askew. "Those are words that could get you killed, Dante," he whispered. "If you go down that path, you won't just be kicked out of the temple. You'll be shunned from society itself. The guards will be on your tail for the rest of your life. Is that something you really want to do? Is this guy worth it?"

I wanted to cry out, to take Calder by the shoulders and shake him. Of *course* Ronan was worth it! But then again, I didn't understand why I felt so strongly about him. After all, we'd only known each other for a handful of days. It seemed downright stupid to give up my entire life and everything I'd ever cared about for some man I'd just met. Sure, he was big and strong, and he made me feel safe, but was that enough? If I managed to get him out of there, spurning my entire life in the process, would he even want me around? Being a werewolf meant he was already always on the run. Would he be willing to accept the additional danger of having a defunct cleric at his side?

Calder continued to gaze in my direction, waiting for an answer. I wasn't sure what to tell him. My heart told me to go after Ronan, but my logic told me to remember my place in the world. As a full cleric, I had certain privileges, but they didn't extend far enough for me to question the laws of Eadronem or the decisions of the Masters. For the first time, I realized the folly of all my hopes and dreams. I'd worked so hard for years to become a cleric, and now that I was one, I realized I was now only *one* step up from the bottom. Even with my new position, I was still living under the heels of the Masters.

"Calder," I said slowly, trying to draw up my courage. "If... If I said he was worth it... Would you help me?"

For a long moment, he was silent, his hands laced in his lap. His foot tapped softly on the ground as he thought, his eyes flicking back and forth. Finally, he took a deep breath and looked up at me once more.

"I... I'll help you," he said at last.

"Oh, Calder! Thank you so—"

"On one condition."

I nodded. "Name it. Anything you want."

"You have to take me with you."

I was a little surprised by his request. "Calder... Why would I leave you behind?"

"I was hoping you'd say that." He slapped his hands on his knees, pushing himself up from the bed. "So, what's the first thing we need to do?"

"This is going to sound crazy."

"Count me in."

I rolled my eyes with a smile. "I-I need to get into Ryker's office."

His eyebrows shot up as his eyes went wide.

"I need to see if what the Goddess said was true," I explained. "Ryker isn't going to admit that he or the other Masters are trying to become immortal. But I have to know. That seems like the most farfetched part of the Goddess' claims. If that turns out to be true, then I'll believe her. And... And I'll accept her offer and become her champion. Not to mention we'll have the evidence to expose him and the other masters."

"And you need me to?"

"To get him out of his office for a little while."

"So you can sneak in."

"So I can sneak in."

Calder placed a hand on my shoulder. "You're fucking crazy; you know that? I don't know what effect this werewolf had on you, but clearly, his dick broke your sanity." A big smile curled across his face. "I like it. And, lucky for you, I've spent my life breaking all the rules, so I've got a guy that I think can get us out of here." He reached into his pocket and withdrew a large silver key. "And I stole a skeleton key off Master Cornelius months ago."

My mouth fell open as I watched him spin the key around his index finger. "I... I don't know what to say..."

"Get me off this gods forsaken island, and I won't even require a thank you."

I nodded. "You have my word."

"Good. Now let's get the fuck out of here."

***

I stood a few feet away, hidden in a small alcove with my back to the stone. Knocking echoed down the hallway as Calder's knuckles rapped on Master Ryker's door. I reached down and touched the shape of the stone in my pocket, making sure it was still there. Calder had one just like it. Once I was done with the office, I'd use it to let him know. After that, things were going to get a little crazy. However, we'd spend most of the day planning our escape, and I felt pretty confident we could pull it off. Thankfully Calder had some contacts in the city that he used to smuggle in goods not allowed in the temple. They were going to get us off Aratis. We just had to figure out how to free the prisoners first.

A moment later, I heard the hinges squeak as the heavy wooden door was pulled open. The voice of Ryker's acolyte echoed down the hallway.

"Yes?"

"Master Cornelius sent me," Calder said, a sense of urgency in his voice. "He says he needs Master Ryker to meet him in the Master's Tower immediately."

"One moment."

The door started to swing closed, but Ryker's voice sounded from within.

"What does he want?" he called, the impatience clear in his tone. Clearly, he'd been in the middle of something. "This isn't another one of his idiotic experiments, is it?"

"I don't know, sir," Calder replied. "He just said it was important."

"Tell him I'll find him later."

"I apologize, sir. I was told not to return without you."

There was a groan and a series of slams from within the room. The acolyte was silent, probably terrified of what Ryker would do. He wasn't known for being the most emotionally stable of people when he was angry. It took everything I had not to sneak a glance around the corner as I heard them exit the room, throwing the heaving door closed behind them.

"This had better be good," Ryker snorted, his heavy boots echoing off the stone floors.

"I assure you, sir, Master Cornelius seemed most insistent."

"Shut up," Ryker retorted. "And lead the way. I don't care to hear anything more from you."

In less than a minute, the sounds of their footsteps faded away. Slowly, I peered around the corner, checking to make sure the coast was clear. The hallway was empty, and I darted toward the door, knowing I only had a handful of minutes to search before Ryker came storming back. Reaching out, I tested the door handle. To my surprise, it turned easily in my grasp. Apparently, Ryker wasn't concerned about anyone getting into his office. That or his acolyte had forgotten to lock it on the way out. Either way, I would take the luck I was given.

I slipped inside the office, shutting the door silently behind me. The room was large, bigger than the one Calder and I shared with two other acolytes at times. Each wall was lined with books, leather tomes containing all manner of clerical knowledge. I wondered what untaught spells existed buried between their pages. I took a step toward the shelves; my hand outstretched before I shook my head. This wasn't the time. I needed to find the proof I was looking for. Learning magic could come later.

Heading for the desk, I began rifling through the papers on top of it. Most of them were nothing but orders for temple supplies, training schedules, classes, and the like. Sheet after sheet was tossed to the floor, and no care was given to cover up my tracks. Ryker was going to know someone was in there anyway, so I might as well make it look like a robbery of some sort. There was no way he'd connect it back to me.

With the top of the desk tossed, I began on the drawers. The top two were mostly supplies, blank sheets of paper, scrolls, stamps, wax, seals, quills, and ink. All of them were of excellent quality and make, but not what I was looking for. The lower drawers were filled with papers, filed away in neat stacks, and labeled accordingly. I found records of the acolytes at the temple, each of them with details of their origins and how they were brought to live amongst the clerics. There were thicker files for those promoted to cleric, including one for myself.

I paused for a moment, looking at the small ink sketch of my face with my information next to it. There were a few hastily scrawled notes in the corner. They looked recently added.

Chosen for Baron An'Cleth's job to clear the mines. Has shown a minute sense of ambition but no extraordinary power. Most likely will not survive the mission.

I wasn't sure if I was offended, betrayed, or both. Ryker had sent me on the mission to clear the mines knowing full well that I might not return. Judging by his notes, it seemed like he didn't even *want* me to come back. I turned back to the page, scanning it for any more of his notes. On the bottom of the page was a stamp in red ink, another note scrawled next to it.

Promoted to Full Cleric.

Showed some hesitation to having monster-races put down. Sympathizing with the enemy after brief contact. Possible flight risk. Keep a watchful eye on this one.

So... Ryker had noticed everything. But 'the enemy'? That seemed a bit ridiculous. There was not a single race of people in all of Eadronem waging war on the clerics. Well, except for the elves, they'd been kicked out of their ancestral home in Orostian. The Clerics of the Twilight claimed they were trying to summon some dark and dangerous power to destroy Aratis. At first, I'd believed them. But now I wasn't so sure.

I tossed the file aside with the others, realizing it did nothing except irritate me. Ryker could think whatever he wanted. I was getting out, and nothing he had stored in my file was going to change that.

It only took me a minute more to clear through the rest of the drawers, and I found myself empty-handed. There was nothing in his desk to incriminate him for the crimes the Goddess claimed. I flopped down in the chair, shuffling through the papers on top of his desk one last time to make sure I hadn't missed anything.

"You gotta help me here, Goddess," I said out loud, shaking my head. "I need more to go on than just hearsay."

I shifted a section of the papers, trying to reach those on the bottom, accidentally sending a large stack toppling over the edge. Cursing to myself, I slipped out of the chair onto my knees, sifting through the mess of papers to try to find some tiny scrap of evidence. It took only a few seconds for me to snort in frustration, knowing I was running out of time. I needed to get out of the office soon if I wanted to keep my head.

With a sigh, I leaned back, sitting on my heels. There was no way I was going to find anything of value in this mess. I'd just have to try to find evidence somewhere else. After all, in a couple of hours, I'd no longer be part of the temple anyway. Maybe someone else would have information, anything that could help me figure out if the Goddess was telling the truth. Although, if I was being honest with myself, I was inclined to believe her anyway. As an acolyte, I heard the terrible things the Masters said about other races of people. I'd even believed them. But now I'd learned the truth, I knew better, and I could stomach their hate no longer.

I turned back toward the desk, and just as I started to pull myself back to my feet, I saw something. It was a small dark leather cylinder attached to the underside of the desk, a button snap on the very end of it. I reached out, pulling the snap free. It came loose easily, revealing a glimmering object within. Curling the tips of my fingers around it, I pulled it free.

It was a wand. But not like any other I'd seen before. Most were made of crystal, the same that came out of the mines down in Terrastera. They were terribly fragile and easy to break. Sometimes they were even consumed by spells should the cleric wielding them go a little too far. However, while this wand gave off the same faint blue glow as the crystal in the mines, it was completely made of silver metal shaped with intricate facets. A large clear crystal gem was set into the base, veins of crystalline ore spiraling up the shaft to the very tip. It lit up in my hand the moment I took hold of it, a pulse of magical power thrumming across my skin. Below me, I heard a faint click.

Glancing down, I saw a small compartment open at the bottom of the desk that hadn't been there before. Still clutching the wand, I leaned down and pulled it open. Inside was a small red leatherbound journal with a golden rune gilded on the cover. I quickly tucked the wand into my robes and flipped the book open. My eyes grew wide as I scanned the first page, then the second. A moment later, I snapped the book shut, quickly shoving it into my robes as well.

I had everything I needed to prove what Ryker was up to now. The Goddess had been telling the truth all along. With the book, I could expose him to the world.

Now I just had to get Ronan and get out alive without getting caught. I pushed myself to my feet, quickly checking to make sure both the book and the wand were secure. Crossing the room, I headed for the door, ready to find Calder and get the hell out of Aratis for good.

The moment I reached out for the door, I watched the latch lift of its own accord, the squeal of hinges making my blood run cold as it opened.

Twenty-Three: Ronan

It had been over a day since I'd been arrested, and still, Dante hadn't come for me. For a long time, I'd held out hope that maybe he'd just been scared, that our sudden arrest had thrown him off guard. But surely, he'd speak with his master and have us set free, right? However, as time slowly ebbed on, so too did my hope.

Dante had abandoned me, abandoned us all.

The very thought caused my chest to seize up, making it hard to breathe. Why the hell had I let that little bastard so far under my skin? What a stupid thing to do. He was a Cleric of the Twilight, after all. That alone should have been enough to keep me on my guard. But there I was, sitting in a stinking dungeon at the bottom of the Twilight Temple, both Torval and Kai sitting in the cell opposite me, and neither of them deserving to be there.

I couldn't help feeling like it was all my fault. Had I fought harder to resist Dante or fought harder to get away from the guards, maybe all of us would be free. But the more I thought about it, the more I realized we'd been fucked from the moment we signed up for that job. The Clerics of the Twilight had set a trap for us; like suckers, we'd fallen for it completely. I should have known such a generous reward wouldn't be honored. Things that seemed too good to be true always were, in fact, too good to be true. It was one of the most basic lessons I'd learned from the Brotherhood, yet I'd let greed overpower my sense of reason. And now I was paying the price for my stupidity.

Not only that, but I'd let myself get close to one of their own, building some fairy-tale relationship with the first pretty face I'd seen. I couldn't deny that I'd been attracted to him from the moment I saw him, even though my gut told me to keep away. He was a dick from the moment we'd met, and yet I pined after him like some love-sick puppy. I managed to resist him for a while, but the magic he performed to bond us was the final straw. After that, I was lost, completely overtaken by his rough charm. It didn't matter how rude he was or what he said. I still wanted to be right next to him, protecting him every step of the way.

And now I was paying for it.

Metal shackles dug into my wrists and ankles, chains running between them to give me just enough mobility to walk but not enough to run or attack. At first, I'd thought I could break out of them by shifting, waiting until I was alone in my cell to attempt it. But the moment I'd started to shift, invisible runes lit up along the metal, each link imbued with binding magic. A painful shock shot through my body, and I reverted back, my shift completely denied. After that, I couldn't even attempt to draw on it, as if my very essence were being subdued by the magic contained within the metal. I was a caged animal, rage and fury building up inside of me. But no matter how angry I became, I couldn't overcome the intense hopelessness that pervaded my soul.

My heart was broken. And what made it even worse was that I knew it was my own fault for being so fucking stupid.

"Back away from your doors!" a voice rang out, echoing throughout the dungeon. "If you want your bread and water for the day, keep to the back wall of your cell!"

I glanced toward the end of the hallway as a pair of guards came down the stone stairs, each of them carrying a small wooden tray with a pitcher and half-burnt loaves of bread balanced on them. They looked irritated that they even had to come down to feed us.

"Get back!" the one in front yelled again, his steel gauntlet ringing as he banged it against the wall to get our attention. "Unless you want a blade between your ribs. We don't mind that, do we?" he said, glancing back at the other guard.

"Not at all," the other replied. "In fact, we'd enjoy a bit o' action round here. Been too damn quiet."

I did as I was told, sulking to the dark shadows in the back of my cell. Had this exchange taken place before my trip into the mines with Dante, I might have begged them to fight me, to see if they had what it took to bring someone like me down. But I was thoroughly and utterly defeated. Instead, I leaned my back against the wall, sinking down with my knees pressed up against my chest and my head hanging toward the floor. Across the hall, I heard Kai and Torval move back as well. They were still following my lead for some reason, although I didn't understand why.

"Aww looks like no fun for us today," the first guard sighed.

"I thought they said these monsters was dangerous?" the second replied.

"Everyone knows Orcs have got dick for brains, so he's probably still trying to figure out what we are," the first said, tossing a tray down in front of the other cell. "And Draak, well, they look tough, but they're about as meek as it comes. Don't get too close, though. I hear they're blood drinkers."

I heard Kai snort in frustration at the guard's words, but to his credit, he didn't say anything. Torval, on the other hand, tried to speak but couldn't get any words out due to his muzzle. The clerics knew he could cast spells, so he'd been bound similar to me, only they magically silenced him as well. Without the ability to move or form words, Torval's magic was inaccessible, making him about as useless as myself.

Another tray hit the ground in front of my cell, but I didn't look up.

"And this one," the first guard said. "This one's nothing but a fuckin' mongrel. Hardly better than a mutt off the street."

"It's true then?" the other asked. "He really is a... a werewolf?"

"Aye. That he is. And a big motherfucker to boot."

"Can ya really turn into one if he bites ya?" There was an eagerness in the guard's voice that couldn't be missed. "Wouldn't mind lookin' like that. Ya see the muscles on this guy?"

"A bite would kill you in a matter of minutes," I replied softly, not looking up at them.

"How the fuck do you know?" he spat back, his gauntlet clanging against the iron bars. "I'm tough! I could survive it!" He scoffed, smacking his hands against his chest as a pathetic show of aggression. "Probably could start some new guard for the clerics too. Have this whole place under my boot."

I chuckled under my breath, no longer giving a fuck what these idiots thought of me. "You wouldn't survive." I lifted my gaze, staring him dead in the eyes. "Nobody like *you* ever survives."

"He's got quite a mouth on him," the first guard said, lifting an eyebrow in my direction. I pulled out a key ring, glancing over at his friend, who was clearly seething. "You wanna fuck him up?"

"Yes..." the other replied, his chest heaving in fury. He drew a dagger from his belt, tapping it against the bars. "I'll show you who's more powerful."

The lock turned easily, and the door swung open, letting the second guard into the cell. He pulled off his helmet, tossing it to the side, his short dark hair sticking out at weird angles. I could already see the fury in his eyes. I'd insulted his pride, one of the worst things you could do to a human man with an ego. He wanted me dead. But I was going to the hangman's noose no matter what, so I didn't care. At least I'd take one of these stupid fuckers along with me. They needed to be taught a lesson anyway.

"Big man," I sneered, staring up at him. "Fighting someone who's bound and unarmed."

His eyes grew wide, his nostrils flaring with anger. "Unshackle him!" he barked at the other.

"You fuckin' crazy?" he replied. "Those manacles stop him from turning into a werewolf! I'm not about to let him fuckin' loose to kill everyone in the entire city!"

The other guard reached back, tearing the keys from his hands. "He's not gonna get out because I'm gonna fuckin' kill him!"

"Give it back!"

"Fuck you!"

Something in me snapped as they started to squabble with one another, each trying to wrestle the keys away. After spending days cooped up underground and having my heart ripped out, I was looking for a way to blow off some steam. The dark-haired guard had turned his back to me, and I saw my opportunity.

Lunging up from the floor, I threw the manacle chain over his head, pulling it tight against his neck. All at once he forgot about the keys, the metal clattering on the stone as his hands tried desperately to pull the chain away from his neck. The other guard stared, looking absolutely dumbfounded, as I slowly choked his co-worker to death.

"So... you thought you could take on a werewolf and live, huh?" I growled in his ear, my voice lower than seemed possible. "Think you'd survive a bite from one of my kind?"

The man tried to respond, but with the chain cutting off his windpipe, all he could manage was a wet gurgle. His face was beet red, several veins in his eyes already popping from the strain.

"Then prove it."

With that, I reared back, opening my jaw wide before clamping down on the side of his neck. Unable to shit, my teeth weren't as sharp as they could be, but it was still easy to break the skin. The metallic tang of blood filled my mouth as I crunched down harder, his muscle and sinew popping as my teeth plunged further into his neck. As soon as I felt like I had a good grip on him, I tore my jaw away, taking a large chunk of flesh along with it. At the same moment, I pulled the chain away, giving the guard a shove.

He fell to his knees in front of me, coughing and choking as he tried desperately to staunch the flow of blood from the gaping wound in his neck. I spat what remained of him in my mouth on the ground, doing nothing to wipe away the blood running down my face.

"You have roughly thirty seconds to live before the curse kills you," I smiled, feeling proud of myself. It would probably mean a more painful death for me in the end, but I didn't care. At least there was one less asshole in the world. "I hope you're ego was well placed."

The moment I finished speaking, the curse began to take effect. The dark-haired man's eyes widened, sweat breaking out all over his body as he went pale. His limbs began to shake, his hands barely able to keep pressure on his wound. He reached out toward the other guard, but he took a step back, clearly worried the curse might spread to him too. A few seconds later, the guard's veins began to blacken, creeping down his neck and across the side of his face. His eyes rolled back, foam forming at the corners of his lips as he started to convulse.

I couldn't help but smile, knowing already that he was doomed. When I'd been turned, I spent the entire night drenched in sweat, writhing in agony until the sun came up, my body cracking, breaking, and reforming over and over until the curse had taken effect. I'd seen several attempts to change people since then, and nobody ever survived the convulsions once they started. It was the body's last attempt to expel the doom within it. And it never worked.

I was so focused on the guard in front of me that I didn't notice the other slip into the cell. By the time I heard the whistle of steel through the air, I knew I couldn't dodge it in time. The blade struck me full in the torso, sinking several inches into my gut. A pained gasp escaped my lips as I fell backward, striking the wall and sinking to the floor. My hand was already pressed to the wound, the heat of fresh blood surprising between my fingers. I didn't have to pull it away to know I was a goner. He'd punctured something vital, the throbbing pain filling my entire body.

"Help!" the guard cried, scooping up the keys from the ground before slamming my cell door shut, his co-worker's body lying lifeless inside.

It would only be a few moments before the entire temple came down on us. I looked across the hall toward Kai and Torval, both of them staring at me unblinking. I furrowed my brows, trying to apologize to them silently. But both shook their heads as if to say there was no need. We all knew the fate in store for us. All I'd done was speed up the sentence.

The sound of boots coming down the stone stairs answered the guard's shouts. A moment later, two figures came into view, both dressed in white robes. I was having a hard time focusing on them, my vision already blurred from the pain, but I knew they were clerics from their dress.

"He... He attacked us!" the guard cried as the figures approached. "He ripped Armstrong's neck out and tried to come after me! Armstrong wanted to fight him, but I told him he shouldn't and—"

"Calm yourself," one of the clerics said, his voice smooth and almost familiar. "Here," he added, pulling something from within his robes. "Let me help you."

The guard was still visibly shaking but nodded his head. I saw the dull glow of white light as the cleric raised something up between them. A moment later, the light changed color, shifting to sudden darkness before the guard's body crumpled to the ground.

Twenty-Four: Dante

"What the fuck?!" Calder cried next to me as I lowered the wand I'd found in Ryker's desk. "What kind of magic was that?"

I sighed. I'd already explained to him what I could do the night before *and* after he'd walked in on me in Ryker's office. In fact, I'd nearly blasted him in the face by mistake. Normal clerics usually weren't dangerous to sneak up on, but I wasn't exactly normal at this point.

"Necromancy," I said, slipping the wand back into my sash. "I told you about it already."

"Yeah! But I haven't *seen* you use it!" He crouched down, poking at the guard lying in a heap on the ground. "Is... Is he dead?"

"Yep."

"Wow. That's crazy."

Shaking my head, I stooped down and took the keys from the guard. I didn't have time to sit there chatting with Calder. I needed to see Ronan and apologize to him. But the moment I looked up into the cell, my gaze came to rest on the blood seeping between his fingers, and I felt all the color drain from my face.

He was hurt. Badly.

"Ronan!" I called out, fumbling with the keys.

After a moment, I managed to shove one of the rusted keys in and turn the lock over. Throwing the door wide, I ran to his side, kneeling as I pulled the wand from my sash.

"Move your hand," I commanded. "I need to see the wound so I can heal you."

But he didn't move.

"Ronan! Move your hand!"

I reached out to pull it away, but I couldn't force him to budge. Even though he was bleeding out in front of me, he still had enough strength to resist my efforts. I glared at him; my teeth clenched in irritation.

"Why... Why are you here?" he asked simply, his eyes going in and out of focus as he stared up at me.

The betrayal in his voice sent an icy spear through my heart.

"I came back to get you," I said, placing my hand on his shoulder and leaning close.

"Why?"

"What do you mean, why?" I scoffed.

He reached out, his fingers gripping the front of my robes. "Tell me."

I sighed, annoyed by his persistence. "I came back because you saved my life. You all did," I said, gesturing to Torval and Kai in the other cell. "It's not right that they're punishing you just for existing. None of you have done anything to deserve this!"

Ronan stared at me for a long moment. "That... That's all?"

My heartbeat quickened, realizing what he wanted me to say. After spending all night telling Calder my story, then hatching and executing a plan, I hadn't had much time to sit down and really dig through my emotions on the subject. I was driven forward by a sense of righteousness, that saving them was the *good* thing to do. It was easy to see that Ryker and the rest of Eadronem were prejudiced for no reason. But as for my personal stakes in the situation... well, I'd completely pushed them aside. It didn't matter why *I* wanted to do it, only that it *should* be done.

"I... I don't know what you want me to say," I replied, trying to pull his arm away once more. "Just let me heal you, and we'll have all the time in the world to talk about things."

"You're still scared, aren't you?" he asked, his voice growing weaker by the second. "After everything we've been through and all the danger you've put yourself in to get here. You still can't admit how... how you feel."

"How I feel is irrelevant," I replied, still trying to pull his arm away, but he was being stubborn. "The only thing that matters is getting you all out of here."

"Then what?" He paused, his dark eyes staring up at me. "Is this just your good deed for the year? A debt to repay to us for protecting you in those mines."

"No, of course not."

"Then what is it?"

"It... It's hard to explain."

Ronan winced in pain as he tried to move, his fingers flexing around his wound that was still bleeding profusely. He was running out of time.

"Just let me help you, and we'll talk," I pleaded. "Please."

"Tell me," he repeated, gritting his teeth.

I leaned in close to him, my hand cupping the side of his face as I stared into his eyes. I knew what he wanted me to say, but I didn't know if I was ready to speak it aloud. Things between us had blossomed quickly in the mines under the stress of fighting to survive. Did that make these roiling emotions in the pit of my stomach valid? I'd been pushing them down over and over, thinking it was just the heat of the moment that spurred them into life. Days had passed by now, and I still felt the same, but then again, we were still fighting for survival. When all this turmoil came to an end, would I still feel the same? Would Ronan even want me once I was no longer off-limits? What blossomed between us was fueled at first by hate. Once the fire was gone, would hate be the only thing left?

"Please," Ronan said softly, his eyes fluttering. "Tell me why."

"Because..." I sighed, trying to gather up all my courage.

It was now or never. Ronan would be gone in less than a minute if I didn't tell him now. Even if I spoke the spell, it might not be enough to save him. I couldn't let him die not knowing the truth just because I was too scared to speak it aloud. He deserved to know how special he was to me, even if what we had lasted only a moment.

"Because... I love you."

The second the words left my lips, I felt his arm go limp, and I pulled it away, jamming the wand down toward his wound. He smiled as his eyes fluttered shut, his chest no longer rising and falling with his breath. Drawing up all the magic I could muster, I spoke the incantation that would save him. The wand in my hand glowed bright white as the magic gathered. And yet, as I watched, the wound did not close.

"Come on," I whispered, forcing more of my own power into the wand. "Come on, Ronan! Don't give up on me now!" There were tears running down my cheeks as I spoke the incantation again. "Come back to me, Ronan. You did it once; you can do it again!"

Still, there was no sign of his wound healing.

"NO!" I yelled, throwing more of my power into the wand. "I'm not giving up on you! I love you too much for this to be the end! Goddess help me, you WILL COME BACK!"

The moment the words left my lips, I felt a pulse of white-hot energy course through my veins, and my entire world exploded into blinding light. However, I didn't close my eyes. Instead, I kept them locked on Ronan, praying with all my might that the magic would work. It *had* to. Now that I'd said those three little words out loud, I couldn't bear the thought of losing him forever, not after we'd come so far together. I'd risked everything for him, and I'd be damned if he wasn't getting on that airship with me.

"I see you've returned," a soothing feminine voice said from behind me.

I didn't have to turn around to find out who it was.

"Goddess, please," I begged. "I need your help. I... I did everything you said. I checked on the Masters, and you were right. They're trying to become immortal. I even found the book where they wrote it out, and I'll show it to the whole world if you want me to! I'll be your champion, your slave, whatever you need... just... just please don't let him die."

"My dear child," she replied, kneeling beside me, the tip of her wand coming to rest on Ronan's chest. "You don't have to give yourself up to me to save him because you already have."

I glance down at him once more, realizing that the Goddess wasn't healing him but merely pointing with her wand toward the wound on his torso. It was completely healed, not even a scar left behind in its place.

"B-But... how?"

"I told you," she replied. "You are far more a cleric than anyone you know. Your gifts come directly from me, and therefore your magic is that much greater." She smiled softly in my direction, her dark hair spilling over her shoulders. "But, if you wish to still become my champion, I will happily walk by your side as you bring the world to rights."

All I could manage was a choked sob. I was completely overwhelmed at that moment, a rush of emotions filling every part of my body. Ronan was going to live, I'd told him I loved him, something I never thought I'd get to say for my entire life, and now the Goddess of the Twilight was kneeling next to me, offering to be my personal magical mentor for the rest of my life. Everything I thought I'd lost was returned to me, and then some. There was only one thing left to do.

"All right," I nodded, tears still streaming down my face. "I'll be your champion."

"So it shall be," she nodded in return.

Before I could utter another sound, the blinding light faded around me, and the dungeon came back into view. I heard the others speak at once, all of them trying to get my attention. However, my eyes never left Ronan. Listening to the sound of my own heart pounding in my chest, I waited for his to rise, his breath returning to his body at last.

One heartbeat passed. Then two.

All at once, Ronan's eyes flashed open as he gasped, his chest expanding once more as he shot straight up. His gaze focused on me, his eyes wide as he heaved great breaths to fill his lungs once more.

"Wha-... What the fuck was that?" he said, his bloody hand still grasping at a wound that was no longer there. "What happened?"

I immediately decked him in the face. A streak of pain shot through my hand, and I tried to shake it out. I'd never hit anyone before, and I was almost certain I did it wrong, but I didn't care. Ronan lifted a hand to his face, rubbing the red spot on his cheek where I'd hit him. A moment later, a small grin pulled at his lips.

"What the *fuck* is wrong with you?!" I yelled, this time hitting him in the shoulder. "You were just gonna sit there being stubborn and let yourself die in front of me? For what?! Just to get me to say what you wanted to hear?"

Ronan caught my fist, yanking me close to him.

"Get off me, you fucking oaf!"

I tried to call him several more names, but my words were cut off as he pressed his lips to mine. For the briefest moment, I tried to fight him off. But I barely got my hands to his shoulders before I melted into him, my arms wrapping around his neck. Passion overtook me, driving out all other concerns from my mind. He was alive, and that was all that mattered.

"You're a fucking idiot," I gasped between kisses. "Stubborn... and stupid."

"I love you too," Ronan replied, taking my anger with a grain of salt. "Thank you for coming back for me. I... I didn't think you would."

My heart was pounding a mile a minute, those three words seeping into my brain and gumming up the gears. I was trying desperately to think of what to say to him, but all that came out was, "I'm sorry."

I leaned back into him again, letting the warmth of his body reassure me that he was still there. He stroked my hair, his touch sending waves of electricity through my body. Just being near him, breathing in his scent, filled me with more joy than I could express. I wanted to be at his side always.

"Don't get me wrong," Calder said, shattering the peace. "I love this, I really do. Touching moment. But there's a ninety-five percent chance that we're going to be swarmed by the guards at any second. So, we need to go."

"Right," I said, shaking my head as I pulled away from Ronan. I tossed the keys to Calder. "You let the others out. I'm gonna disintegrate these manacles."

"With what?" Ronan asked, an eyebrow lifted in disbelief. "They're unbreakable. I tried."

I held up the wand, the crystalline veins glowing as they wove their way through the metal. "I stole this from a Master of the temple." I tapped him on the nose with it. "And I'm now the chosen champion of the Goddess of the Twilight. Don't underestimate me."

Ronan's eyes held a hilarious amount of confusion as he tried to process everything I'd said. I just smiled confidently and placed the tip of the wand on the manacles, drawing up the magic to turn them to dust.

"Brace yourself," I said. "This is a made-up spell, so hopefully, it doesn't kill us both."

"Oh fuck..." Ronan muttered.

"Hold on," I said and uttered the incantation.

Twenty-Five: Ronan

By some miracle, we made it out of the temple without being seen and with everyone intact after Dante's experimental magic. I still didn't know what to think of all his talk about being a champion of the goddess, but I figured he'd have time to explain it *after* we made it off Aratis with our lives. Somehow, he'd managed to not only free me from the magical binds that the clerics had placed on me to suppress my werewolf abilities, but he'd also freed Torval from his anti-magic bindings. Both were a great boon because I didn't believe we were going to make it off Aratis without a fight. Although, according to Dante's shifty friend Calder, he'd already booked us secret passage on a ship leaving the sky port in the next ten minutes.

We just had to get there in time.

But sneaking through the streets of Aratis without being noticed was easier said than done. Kai, Torval, and I all looked incredibly out of place; our tattered clothing and unkempt visages were a stark contrast to the prim and perfect nobles that walked the streets. Even the servants that hustled about shot us strange glances, knowing immediately that we didn't belong. But there was no time to keep to be concerned about it. Time was running out, and our only option was to hustle through the open streets in broad daylight. The airship was departing at dusk, and with the sun already kissing the horizon, I knew we were cutting it close.

"Come on!" Calder cried from the front of the group, pointing toward the sky port hanging out over the edge of the floating island. "This is our only shot off this rock!"

In the distance, I could just make out the ship we were meant to take. It was hardly more than a small schooner used to ferry goods to and from Terrastera below. But that meant it was light, fast, and didn't require an entire crew to keep it moving. Even if the larger ships were to give chase, we'd outrun them easily. Once out of sight of Aratis, we could hide away until they gave up the search. It was already pretty clear that the Temple of the Twilight was going to come after us, especially since two of their guards were dead and one of their own had robbed and betrayed them. But we'd be long gone by the time they figured it all out.

I glanced over at Dante, running along beside me. He was breathing hard but keeping pace with us somehow. Kai and Torval were ahead, their legs much longer than the humans guiding us. Calder managed to stay ahead, calling out directions as we went.

"Almost there!" he cried as we neared the sky port at last.

The ship's sails were being lowered, the crystals mounted at the edges of the deck already glowing. The air thrummed with magic as they revved into life, preparing to set sail and leave the city behind. Onboard I could make out a couple of crew and what I assumed was the captain at the helm. Even with the distance, I saw their cat-like ears and the dark fur blowing in the wind. All at once I understood why they were so willing to help us.

However, the moment our feet hit the wooden planks of the docks, a single man stepped out in front of us, cutting off our path. All of us came skidding to a halt. Dante slipped next to me and slammed into the railing at the edge of the walkway. Instinctively I reached out and grabbed him by the back of the robes, pulling him close. I held him close to me as he gulped, realizing that nothing lay beyond the edge of the docks but open air. The trip down to Terrastera from there would be a short, albeit deadly one.

"I should have known," the man said, his voice echoing over the wind. "I thought maybe you harbored some ill will toward the temple, but really Dante. This is quite foolish."

I turned my attention back to the man in front of us, his white robes whipping in the breeze that split over the edge of Aratis. He was tall and muscular with dark hair and a beard that was far too groomed and perfect. At his side, he held a crystalline staff easily as tall as he was.

The setting sun behind him caught the crystal, rainbows shimmering over the ground as the facets split the light into its many colors.

"Get out of our way, Ryker!" Dante called back. "I'm not gonna sit by anymore while you and the other Master's shame the name of the Goddess and her teachings! We won't hesitate to kill you if you don't stand down!"

"My, my," Ryker mused, a smirk forming as he spoke. "You've grown quite the pair on your little trip through the mines. If I'd known this is what it took to have you show some backbone, I would have sent you long ago." He turned toward Calder, his smirk turning to a grimace. "And you. You're just a useless troublemaker, aren't you? No talent, no ambition, and no use to anyone but yourself."

With a muttered word and a casual flick of his staff, Calder was struck full in the chest with a ball of glowing blue light, energy coalescing around his body. The magic lifted him off his feet and threw him backward, where he crashed into Kai, both of them tumbling to the dock. Their bodies slid to the edge, the upper half of Calder's body hanging over the vast nothingness, only clouds floating lazily by below him. Kai grabbed him by the robes, hauling him back up to safety.

I felt Dante bristle beside me, the attempt on his best friend's life striking him down to his core. Ryker obviously didn't care whom he hurt as long as he stopped us from leaving Aratis. I hadn't expected much hesitation, but striking a fellow cleric first surprised me nonetheless. I thought he'd go for me and the others, trying to turn his own against them. But that didn't seem to be the case.

But before I could say anything, Torval stepped between us, his hands held in a casting position. He muttered words under his breath, balls of flame erupting in the air around him. Energy flowed out of his body, filling the air with crackling heat like that of dozens of bonfires all at once. Ryker merely watched, not making any move to stop him. With another wave of his hands, the fires coalesced into one giant fireball hovering a few feet above Torval's head. A simple flick of his fingers sent the massive inferno zipping through the air directly at Ryker's head.

He didn't dodge, move, or even look away from the oncoming attack. Instead, he merely smiled.

The fireball exploded around him, engulfing the entire dock in a sudden burst of flame. The rope railings caught fire along with the masts of two smaller sloops on either side of Ryker. Wooden boards were scorched black, but the fire wasn't long-lived enough to take hold there. The conflagration roared, and for a moment, I thought Ryker must have been consumed by it, turned into nothing but ash and dust. Torval slowly sunk to his knees, the remainder of his magical energies used up and taking a toll on his body. He smiled for a moment, confident that the spell had done its job. But a moment later, his smile faded.

The breeze drove the last of the flames away, and left standing in its wake was Ryker, completely untouched, his robes still as white as they had been only a moment before. I stared in disbelief, my jaw hanging slack. With a simple tap of his staff, the air around him shimmered, and an invisible sheen of magical glass shattered. It wasn't until that moment that I realized Ryker was standing in a perfect circle of untouched wood. He'd blocked the flames without uttering a syllable, which seemed impossible. All around him, masts burned, their canvas licked by flame. Behind him, I saw our own means of escape, the side scorched by the magical fire while the deckhands still cowered, scared for their lives.

"Pathetic," Ryker sneered, glaring down at Torval. "The guards told me you were a great Draak mage that gave them so much trouble. I'm sorry to say the bindings I sent down for you were far too powerful for someone with such *meager* talents."

"That's enough," I snapped, stepping forward as I shook out my arms, trying to get the soreness from the manacles to cease. "We're leaving this hellhole, and you're not going to stop us."

"Ah. The werewolf," Ryker murmured. "I've heard about you. You've got a bit of a temper on you and a clever mind. It turned out to be a deadly combination for my guards, not that you're to be congratulated on that small victory. They're about as stupid as they come."

"And you'll be next," I growled back, my pupils dilating as the irises turned to gold once more.

"Tell me," he said, glancing toward Dante. "How did you ensnare one of my proteges so quickly? I trained him myself, you know. He's quite the talent, and up until your little foray through the mines, he was compliant and, frankly, easy to manipulate. He accepted everything I said without question." He took a step closer, his staff tapping on the dock as he walked. "What is so *appealing* about you that he would give all that up?" He looked me up and down. "Please tell me it's more than just your appearance."

"Not that it's any of your business," I snarled. "But we're bound together. Fated for one another. I didn't know what it was at first, but now I realize it was fate all along."

"He gave you the blessing, didn't he?"

I opened my mouth to retort, but no words came out.

"The Blessing of the Twilight..." Ryker turned to Dante, clicking his tongue. "You silly boy, I told you that should only be used on humans. That was the first lesson of foundational cleric magic. Monsters like *this* can have negative side effects from the blessing. They start getting *ideas* about things, and it can get quite messy." Ryker turned back to me, a cruel smile pulling at his lips. "That connection you feel? The one you so desperately cling to for some semblance of acceptance and belonging? It's not real. Just a lingering after-effect of the blessing. It'll fade in time, and both of you will realize just how foolish you're being."

"I don't believe you," I growled. "He told me how he feels!"

"Dante cannot tell the truth until he's no longer under the influence of the blessing."

I glanced back at Dante, searching his eyes for any sign that what Ryker claimed was true. All I was met with was confusion and fear.

"But thankfully, there's a simple answer," Ryker added, taking another step forward. "Once you're dead, the magic will fade, and both of you will be sane again." He pointed the staff in my direction, the end of it hovering a few inches from my chest. "It's the least I can do."

Before I could react, he muttered a single word under his breath, and a great force struck me in the chest. There was a flash of bright white light as pain wracked my body. I felt my feet come off the ground, and I sailed backward through the air, striking hard cobblestones as I was thrown completely out of the sky port. My head hit the street, and stars erupted into my vision, filling the world with swirling colors and masses. No matter how much I tried, I couldn't focus on anything. The edges of my vision began to tunnel, and I could feel the tell-tale signs of unconsciousness creeping up on me.

I hadn't even gotten a chance to attempt to shift, my one shot taken from me with a few simple words that sowed the seed of doubt in my mind. I hoped against all hope that Ryker was lying, that what Dante had told me was the truth. Once I was dead, would Dante really forget all about me? Did he love me at all? Even I knew that our relationship had blossomed quickly, almost alarmingly so. But I didn't want it to be false. My heart told me it was true, but once again, my mind didn't agree. However, there was a more pressing question on my mind as the sound of boots and clanking staff approached me.

Would I live long enough to find out the truth?

Twenty-Six: Dante

I watched in horror as Ronan's body struck the ground and lay still for the third time. My mind was reeling as Ryker passed me by, a cruel smile still fixed on his lips. Had his words been true? Could the blessing really cause such a strange extended bond between monster and human? I searched my memories, trying desperately to find the lesson Ryker had spoken of. But the harder I searched, the more it slipped like sand through my fingers. I couldn't recall anything from those early lessons, not even the teacher who'd been present at the time.

My eyes focused once more on Ronan as I saw his fingers twitch, his body trying to shift instinctively to right itself. He was dazed and completely out of it while Ryker continued to approach. His crystalline staff rang against the stone as he walked, each tap of his boots signaling another moment closer to Ronan's death should he make it to his side. I knew I had to act, but I wasn't sure what to do. My heart was driving me forward, but the doubt in my mind held me back. Did I really feel the things I thought I did? What if everything with Ronan had been a mistake? Could such a thing be true?

I turned away for a moment, looking out toward the western horizon as the sun slipped halfway down, marking the peak of twilight. Desperately I searched my mind, trying to figure out my next move. Ryker had sown the seeds of doubt, and for a moment, I wasn't sure if the truth in my heart was the truth in my mind.

Before I could overthink or question things further, the sun flashed, drawing my gaze upward. The breeze suddenly stopped, all sounds of the docks and the fight ceasing to exist. I looked about, noticing all of them were frozen in time, the scene around me completely still. However, a familiar voice rang in my ears.

"Don't doubt your heart," the Goddess said.

I glanced around, looking for any hint of her, but there was none. I turned my face back to the sun, the shifting rays of light coinciding with her words.

"Even after everything you've learned, Ryker is still manipulating you. Don't trust him." The amber twilight shifted, glimmering across everything around me. "You've come so far and sacrificed so much to save your love. Don't let it go to waste."

"W-What should I do?" I replied, my voice shaking. "Ryker's too strong. I don't stand a chance against him."

"Sometimes the most powerful of people are the most careless," she said softly. "They turn their backs on those whom they don't consider a threat, and therein lies their greatest weakness."

"You... You mean me..."

"Yes."

"You... You're asking me to *kill* him?"

"I'm asking you to protect what's important to you," she replied simply. "Ryker has disrupted the balance. The proof is in your pocket. Do what you must to stop him from disrupting it further."

"He's not going to stop... unless..."

"Then you already have your answer. Use the power I gifted to you as you see fit. Save Ronan or serve Ryker. That is the choice that lies before you."

I paused for a long moment. "I-I don't know if I'm r-ready for this."

"Few are who find themselves in such circumstances." The light from the sun began to fade as the world around me began to turn once more. "Now is your time to choose. There is no going back. Save the man you love, or let your old master kill him. Fate will have her pound of flesh this day either way."

The sunlight faded as the breeze came back, the sun itself dipping completely below the horizon. The sounds of flapping canvas and the cries of deckhands hit my ears once more.

"W-Wait!" I cried.

But she was gone, and the twilight with her. Now I was on my own, left with a decision that I didn't feel ready to make. However, the sound of Ryker's boots brought me back to my senses, and I spun around to face him. I hesitated for only a moment as he came to stand in front of Ronan.

"You are far more pathetic than I expected," Ryker jeered, jamming the blunt end of his staff into Ronan's chest. "So many fear your kind, and yet I find you hardly more problematic than an excited puppy tripping over his own ears. Quite sad, really."

Ryker raised a hand, and all at once, I sensed magic welling up around him. He was going to strike Ronan down once and for all, just like the Goddess had said. Instinctually I reached inside my robes, withdrawing the wand I'd stolen from his office. My feet carried me across the dock of their own accord. Fear, anger, and pain welled up in my body, filling every inch of me with fury.

How *dare* Ryker send me into the mines like a sacrificial lamb? Even when he was so convinced of my uselessness, he thrust me into danger. He fed me lie after lie for years, only for them to be shattered the moment I was out of his presence. Then he arrested my friends and protectors, putting them up for execution for crimes they didn't commit and laws that had no business being upheld. And while upholding the worst of laws, he bent others for himself, working in secrecy to make sure that they no longer applied to him. He was insane, a danger to the world.

No, it wasn't just Ryker that was the problem. It was the temple itself and all of Eadronem. The world had gone crazy long ago. So much so that the gods had seen it necessary to intervene and name their own champions to set it right. Ryker was a small piece in a much larger puzzle, but I wasn't about to let him take away the only thing that mattered to me in all the world.

"Time to say goodbye, mongrel," Ryker growled, lifting his staff once more. The magic around him swirled, the staff glowing as its blunt end sharpened to a razor point. "I'm only sorry that I couldn't spend a little bit more time studying you. Your species could have been very useful for my future plans." He shrugged. "Oh well. I'll just find another. Farewell, *beast*."

My hand came to rest on Ryker's shoulder, and he hesitated for a moment, turning to face me.

"What the fuck do you want?" he barked. "I told you to stay ba—"

But no more words left his lips as I jammed the wand into the roof of his mouth and released the necromantic magic that had built up inside of me.

His body seized up, the staff still held in midair, ready to strike Ronan through the heart. Ryker's eyes grew wide as he stared down at me, the capillaries in his eyes turning black. He attempted to speak, but the flesh of his mouth had already turned necrotic from where the tip of the wand was jammed. The darkness spread across his features like ink running across his skin. With each second that passed by, more of his flesh died, his blood coagulating in his veins. He had only seconds to live.

"You will *NOT* touch my wolf," I snarled. Leaning in close, I grabbed him by the collar so that we were face to face. "The Goddess of the Twilight is most disappointed in you."

With that, I pushed him backward. He stumbled, his limbs stiff from the necrosis. The staff fell from his hands, shattering into a million pieces the moment it struck the stone, the magic within it vanishing in a flash. For a moment, I thought Ryker would merely collapse on the cobblestones, dead as a doornail. Instead, the momentum of his body carried him back to the edge of the docks. He fell, his body striking the wooden boards, bouncing once, and slipping over the side of Aratis, plummeting to the world far below.

I knew I should feel bad for what I'd done to him, but the moment his body vanished from my sight, I felt nothing but relief. My liar and manipulator was gone from my life and all his plans with him. The journal in my pocket held all the evidence I needed to let the world know how terrible the Masters of the temple were. Hopefully, now that one of them was out of the way, it would put a damper on their plans for immortality. However, that realization came with another. If the Masters had been lying about all of that and covering up their secrets, what else lay out there in the world for us to uncover? It was a daunting thought, but one I pushed away.

That worry was for another day.

Slipping the wand back into my sash, I kneeled down next to Ronan and placed a hand on his chest and the other on his forehead. He still looked dazed, blood soaking the back of his head where he'd struck the stone street. Muttering a few words under my breath, I felt a familiar heat rise up in me, trickle down my arms and into his body. The holy light of the Goddess flowed through me, healing all of his wounds in a matter of seconds.

Ronan's eyes cleared, and he stared up at me. His expression was one of confusion and doubt, but I simply traced my fingers across his jaw, cupping his cheek.

"It's not true," I whispered. "The bond isn't what made me love you. It... It was just you."

The dark brown of Ronan's eyes shifted to gold in an instant as a smile spread across his face. Without a word, he pulled me down close, pressing his lips to mine. With a simple touch, I was removed out of space and time, nothing existing in all of Eadronem but Ronan and the touch of his skin against my own. I wanted it to last forever, but the shouting of others on the docks brought us back to reality.

"Let's go," I whispered, pulling away from him. "Some place nobody knows who we are. And let's.... let's do some good in this world, huh?"

"I'll follow you anywhere," Ronan replied, his golden eyes glowing. "You're my home. Wherever you go, I go."

"Come on, you two!" Calder cried behind us. "The airship is leaving! RIGHT NOW!"

"Looks like we've got a boat to catch," Ronan smiled. He started to push himself to his feet, taking my hand for support. "As soon as we're on land, I need a new sword and some armor. If being around you is going to be this dangerous, I'll need to be well-equipped."

I glanced down at his crotch, then back up, giving him a small wink. "You're already well equipped, but we'll get you a sword."

"FLIRT LATER! SHIP! NOW!" Calder yelled.

"Fly away with me?" I said, holding out my hand.

His reply was simple. "Always.

Epilogue: Dante

Months had passed, seemingly in the blink of an eye. In that time, Ronan and I had managed to flee Terrastera and cross the ocean northward to the port town of Turmarca. From there, we turned northeast, trekking our way across the northern lands, taking jobs as we went. I'd done my best to keep a low profile after killing Master Ryker, but to my knowledge, the Temple of the Twilight had yet to put out a bounty on my head. I had an idea that it had something to do with the journal still in my possession, the incriminating evidence that could bring them all down. But I wasn't holding out hope that it would last forever.

That's why we were always on the move, never staying in one place for longer than a few days. It was a tough life and definitely not what I was used to. We'd left many friends behind, including Kai, Torval, and Calder. All of them had gone their separate ways eventually, splitting off toward their own destinies.

Calder actually stayed with us all the way to Jyra, going no further once he found his family, who were understandably excited to see him. We'd stayed there for a few days with him, getting to know them and sleeping in their barn for the night. It was a wonderful little farm, but eventually, we knew we had to keep moving. Calder knew he couldn't stay for long either, having a hunch that the clerics would know where to find him if they came looking. Instead, he convinced his family to sell their farm and leave, staying with them just long enough to help them with the move.

We'd parted on a foggy autumn morning, the mist shrouding us from discerning eyes. I was devastated to leave my best friend behind, but with Ronan at my side, I knew I'd be okay. Calder would get his family to safety, and hopefully, he could have a life of his own as well. They'd planned to follow our tracks back to Turmarca and start a new life there, away from prying eyes.

Ronan and I bounced our way across the landscape as winter set in, going from village to village offering our services. Northeast of Jyra, we aided a druid village near the edge of a great lake. We helped them rid their forest of a terrible hairy beast that had come down from the northern mountains and taken up residence nearby. It had proven to be quite a feat, even with the combined strength of Ronan and myself. But after days of tracking and preparing for the fight, we were successful. And the druids, to our surprise, offered us a home of our own to overwinter in as thanks for our deeds.

We accepted gladly, knowing that the company of the druids was not only friendly but that they would never sell us out to the clerics. The Temple of the Twilight had made it their personal mission to give the druids a bad name, calling them 'witch doctors' and 'graceless healers'. It was true that their magic was more natural, with a tendency to leave scars, but that didn't mean it was less effective. Cleric magic left no trace, but we didn't possess the skills to diagnose and treat normal diseases. In fact, most clerics avoided anyone with common ailments unless they had the coin to make it worth their attention. The druids, however, helped anyone, whether they had coin or not.

And so, we spent a long northern winter together in our small hut, a fire blazing as we enjoyed a hard-won peace that we knew wouldn't last forever. The winds howled outside as snow drove down from the mountains, but inside, everything was warm and cozy. Every day was one of exploration as Ronan, and I got to know one another more than we'd ever done with anyone else. There were long hikes through a snow-covered forest, the white powder so deep in places that we'd have to turn back to the village. The druids taught us their ways of collecting herbs and food during the colder months, while Ronan hunted to provide meat in return.

It was an easy and simple way of life, one that I'd grown all too fond of when the snow began to recede and spring came once more. Eventually, the time arrived when the druids began to plan their trip back south through the forest. They spent their summers near Jyra, selling their wares and tending to their lands there to raise crops. Soon Ronan and I would have to leave. Although we knew we'd stayed in one place for too long, we were still reluctant to go. The road would hold many wonders, but peace like what we'd experienced there wouldn't be one of them.

One particularly warm night, Ronan and I decided to take a walk after sunset, enjoying the woods one last time. Tomorrow the druids were leaving, and we had no choice but to part ways with them as well. All around us, the forest was filled with birdsong as they came to roost for the night, their nests already built. The buds on the trees had broken a few days before, the first signs of new leaf growth catching the warm breeze. On the edges of the path, early spring blooms pushed up from the forest litter, filling the air with their sweet scent. It was a beautiful place to be, even if it was about to come to an end.

We walked hand in hand along the path to the top of a low hill covered in dense woods. On the western side was a small break in the trees, leaving a sun-drenched hillside where we could sit in the fresh grass and feel the warmth on our faces. Ronan sat down with his back to a tree. I took my favorite place between his legs, leaning back against his chest, his arms draped over me. There in his arms, I felt safe and protected, the sun warming my skin and filling my nostrils with his masculine scent.

"I wish we could stay here forever," I sighed, pulling his arms tighter around me. "This place is a dream come true."

"It is," Ronan replied. "But, like all dreams, it has to come to an end eventually."

I sighed again. "I know." I turned my head, glancing up at him. "What are the chances that they're never going to come looking for us?"

"Not good," he said, shaking his head. "I'm sure they've already been looking for us."

"But we haven't heard anything about it. Nobody even knows that Master Ryker is dead."

"Because they know if they announce it to the public, it'll drive us away." He rubbed his big hands across my chest, trying his best to comfort me. "The Clerics of the Twilight have always been masters of keeping their intentions hidden until the last moment. You've seen that in action, and I've seen several members of the Brotherhood fall prey to their methods."

"I know... I just... I guess I just had delusions about having a semi-normal life."

"You're fucking a werewolf," Ronan chuckled. "How normal did you think it was going to get?"

"You're right, I know... Being the champion of the Goddess isn't helping, either. There's things she wants me to do, to set right in this world that I've been putting off."

"She can forgive us one winter," Ronan said, squeezing me close. "The world will keep on turning either way. Besides, if she wants you around for the long haul, we'll have to be careful and methodical about how we do things. We can't just waltz into the next big town and announce the entire order of clerics are bastards."

"True," I nodded. "It'll have to be more subtle than that. Something that gets through the people without being so loud that it becomes a target."

"Like a rumor?" Ronan asked.

"Yeah. That seems about right." I looked up at him. "Do you know someone that can help us?"

"I... I might."

"Who?"

He looked at me for a long moment, clearly battling against himself.

"Just say it," I said. "I'm open to all suggestions. We gotta start somewhere."

"I think... maybe the Brotherhood could help us," he said at last. "They're based in Cahl. We could go there."

I felt my jaw go slack. "W-would they? Is that something they do?"

He shrugged. "I mean, they've been helping shifters under the radar for centuries now and keeping more dangerous ones, like mine, under control. If there's one group of people that's good at getting things done without being seen, it's them."

"But... would they be willing to help someone like me?" I swallowed hard. "W-with my background?"

"You've got me," he smiled, kissing me on the back of the head. "I'll vouch for you."

"Will that be enough?"

"I don't know. But it won't hurt to try."

"They won't try to take me out or anything?"

Ronan stared at me; one eyebrow lifted. "I'd like to see them try with me around." He turned me around, lifting me to his lap easily so my legs were wrapped around his waist. "I would do anything to protect you. If I had to crawl through hot coals on my hands and knees to save you, I would do it. You are everything to me, Dante."

I felt my face flush bright red immediately, my cock twitching in my pants at his words. "Y-you know what talk like that does to me...."

He pulled me close, pressing our lips together for a long passionate kiss. I melted into him, opening up to let his tongue swirl around my own. There was a telltale throb against my butt as he grew hard under me. His kisses always left me breathless, the hunger in them sapping me of all resistance I had toward his wiles. Not that I had much to begin with.

"I'm counting on it," he said at last, giving me a small wink. His eyes had turned gold already. "I love you."

I shook my head. "I love you too, you big oaf."

His cock throbbed against my ass again, sending a tingle up my spine.

"Should we head back to the village?" I asked, well aware of what we were both craving.

"Not this time," he replied, kissing his way down my neck and shoulder as he pulled my robes aside. "You won't have to keep yourself quiet out here." He nibbled the lobe of my ear, drawing out a hiss of satisfaction. "It's been too long since I heard you let go."

His words had such a profound effect on me, and my body reacted to him instantly. I shrugged my robes off my shoulders, exposing my skin to the warm sunlight and his touch. Between his words, his thick scent, and the touch of his lips, there was no way I could resist him. He'd learned all too quickly that I had no resistance when it came to him. Whatever he wanted to do to my body was fine with me. I welcomed it.

And, just like almost every night since we'd come to that winter forest, I gave in once more.

Reaching down, Ronan pulled my sash away, tucking them off to the side gently with the metallic wand I carried. With that gone, my robes fell open easily, my lithe form exposed for his viewing pleasure. I loved the way he drank me in with his eyes like he was seeing me for the first time. I'd never felt more beautiful than when he looked at me like that. But the hunger behind his gaze, that was what really drove me wild. I leaned forward, playing my cheek against his.

"Take me," I whispered into his ear. "I'm all yours."

I didn't need to ask twice.

Ronan's fingers slipped under my robes, pushing them off the rest of the way. My throbbing cock bounced free as he lifted me up and out of them. Placing my feet on the ground, he grabbed my hips, his large hands spreading across my ass and squeezing as he pulled me forward. Before I even had a moment to process what was going on, my cock plunged into his open mouth, his tongue rolling sensually over my crown and making me shudder.

"Fuck!" I hissed through my teeth. "Warn a guy next time!"

A low chuckle vibrated across my shaft, but that was all I got out of him. With one hand on my ass, Ronan used the other to slowly work off his own trousers, peeling the leather down without missing a beat with his lips. His mouth was warm and soft, and he was an artist with his tongue. I'd never met anyone quite as talented as him when it came to sucking cock. There were several mornings I'd woken up already inside his mouth, and it had quickly become one of my favorite things. Getting drained before sunup was a great way to start the day.

Before I knew it, Ronan had kicked off his trousers, and both of his hands were back on my ass, spreading my cheeks as he worked his lips up and down my shaft. I had one hand on his head, my fist balled up in his hair, guiding him back and forth at my preferred pace. He made no complaints, easily following my instructions with precision. I arched my neck back, staring up at the sky, moans escaping my lips with every passing second. He was too good at this, and with his thick fingers making slow circles around my hole, he was getting me dangerously close to the edge.

"Time to switch," I said, glancing down at his throbbing beast of a cock between his legs. "I don't want to blow yet."

"Good idea," he growled, pulling away from my cock with a small popping sound.

However, instead of letting me get to my knees as I planned so I could service him, he spun me around and grabbed my hips once more, forcing me to lean forward in front of him. A second later, I felt myself go limp as his hot tongue began to caress my hole.

"Oh gods..." I moaned, leaning forward to give him easier access. He had a hold of my thighs, easily keeping me in an upright position without my help. "Fuck that feels good..."

Again, another satisfied growl echoed through my body, this time vibrating against my entrance and sending shivers up my spine. Ronan was serious this time. Getting this much attention only meant one thing. He wanted to knot me. And with his tongue swirling around my hole, I felt myself getting looser and looser by the second. I wanted him inside me, for him to fill me up with his seed. As his mate, it was my duty to be bred by him as often as possible, or at least that's what I told myself. I had a feeling I might've been just a little bit of a slut, especially where Ronan was concerned.

His tongue moved up and down, teasing at my hole before I felt a small nibble on my cheek. The little tinge of pain felt amazing, setting all my nerves on fire in the best way possible. Between my legs, I could see Ronan's cock throbbing, thick precum leaking down his shaft and glimmering in the sunlight. I reached a hand down, gathering some of it up on my finger before bringing it to my lips.

"Mmm," I hummed. "You taste amazing."

There was a muffled reply from between my cheeks, but I didn't understand what he said. But judging by his increase in tenacity, I figured it was a good thing. Long strokes of his tongue were followed by short flicks and deep swirls around my ring. After only a few minutes, I could tell my body was ready to take his massive girth. All winter, I'd been practicing, and I'd gotten used to his monster-sized cock. It still wasn't easy, and I figured it never would be, but I loved how he felt inside me, filling me up more than I ever thought possible.

"I can't wait any longer," I huffed, my breath ragged from all the moans escaping my body. Turning around, I sat back down, straddling his hips. "Please," I whispered, leaning forward so that my slick hole slid over the head of his cock. "Take me."

There was no hesitation as Ronan angled his hips, holding me tightly as he pressed the head of his cock against my hole. I felt the deep rumble in his chest more than I heard it, his entire body vibrating underneath me. He slowly began to rock his hips back and forth, grinding his thick manhood against me. I leaned forward, moaning into his neck as his crown slowly opened me up, each stroke letting him in a little further.

"Fuck yes," he growled, his fingers spreading my cheeks wider to accommodate his massiveness. "I want to hear every delicious noise you make as I breed you."

"Yes, sir," I moaned back, feeling his cock slide a little further inside.

With one last push, I felt his head slide past my ring at last. After that, the rest of his shaft came easily as he slowly lowered me down. Already his thickness filled me up until all I could see were stars. The world around me melted away. All that was left was his touch, his scent, and the throbbing inside my body. I let out a shaky breath as I came to rest against his half-formed knot. The easy part was done. His knot would be the challenge, but it wasn't one I was going to lose. Maybe I had more determination than was good for me, but I never fell down on the job when it came to giving Ronan everything he wanted from me.

"Fuck... you feel so fucking good," Ronan mumbled, leaving a trail of kisses down my neck and shoulder. "You take me better than anyone else ever has."

"Good," I replied, giving him a small smirk. "And I plan on taking it all."

A low growl met my words as I leaned back, my hole stretching even further. Ronan knew the drill. He'd have to fuck me if he wanted his knot inside me. My ass wasn't going to stretch itself. With his thick fingers wrapped around my waist, Ronan began to slowly work me up and down in tandem with his hips, his beastly cock plunging deeper and deeper into my body with each thrust. His ridge bumped over my prostate with each stroke, sending waves of ecstasy through my body. Already my cock was leaking precum all over Ronan's belly as it rubbed against his skin, creating just the right amount of friction.

"Fuck you feel amazing," Ronan growled after a minute or two, the speed of his pounding increasing. "I'm already getting close."

"Don't stop," I replied, my arms wrapped around his neck as I arched my back, my face looking up at the sky. "I beg you..."

My words did the trick. I felt Ronan's body tense beneath me as he evened out his pace, making sure to push me a little further with each thrust. Already his knot was stretching me out, each stroke letting a little bit more of it in until I knew it would only take a little push to go the rest of the way. As my hole struck his knot once more, I paused, letting my weight rest against it. My tunnel widened to accommodate his girth, and with a wave of pleasure, I felt myself sink the rest of the way down, his knot fully buried inside me.

"Oh fuck," Ronan groaned, his grip tightening around my waist. "Fuck I'm close."

"Me too," I replied breathlessly between moans. "Breed me... please..."

Ronan's movements were jerky, but he continued to rock his hips back and forth nonetheless. His knot ground against my prostate, filling my body with the most intense pleasure I'd ever felt in my life. Each movement pushed him a little deeper, my ring creating a seal between us as his knot thickened inside me. I could feel the orgasm building in my belly, the warm sensation spreading through my balls and up the shaft of my cock as I rocked back and forth, hungry for every inch he could give me.

"F-Fuck," I gasped. "I'm gonna..."

"Fuck... me too..."

My abs tensed, and my balls drew up as the floodgates burst. I cried out, arching my back even further as I came. My cock throbbed against Ronan's chest as I shot my load, covering his chest and neck in thick ropes of cum. At the same time, I felt his knot pulse inside me, Ronan's entire body tensing under my touch. With a deep growl, he pushed me down, forcing his knot further into my body as he came over and over again, the heat of his seed filling my belly.

For several seconds we stayed there, both of us gasping for air as our tandem orgasm subsided, the last drops of cum leaking out of us both. All at once, I felt the strength leave my body, and I collapsed against him. For several long minutes, we stayed there, forgetting about the mess between us or the world we lived in. There was nothing but Ronan and I in that moment, one with each other and in our own little world. The heat of the setting sun against my skin felt nice as he wrapped his arms around me, holding me close. Our hearts beat as one, the seconds passing by in silent peace.

"Th-thank you," I managed to say eventually. "Thank you for always taking such good care of me. For protecting me."

"I'll always protect you," he replied, placing a soft kiss against my neck. "I love you more than anything in this whole wide world."

I smiled, feeling the warmth of his words spread throughout my entire body.

"I love you too."

Sneak Peek: Dragon's Redemption

The transformation magic was wearing out, but I still hadn't cum yet. I gripped the courtesan's hips tighter, increasing the speed of my pounding. Flesh slapped together, the man in front of me moaning like a bitch into the pillow. I couldn't tell if he was enjoying it or not, but it didn't matter. He'd been paid well for his service and was a means to an end. Besides, he should count himself lucky. My spell made my body look and feel human. If I were in my true form with ridges and scales running down my cock, he probably wouldn't be as comfortable.

Or maybe he'd like it more. I didn't know, and I didn't care. What mattered right now was cumming. That's what I paid for, and that's what I was going to get.

Digging my fingers into his hips, I increased my speed, the sound of our flesh slapping together filling the room as the bed banged against the wall. I didn't care who heard me. It was the middle of the day anyway. Anybody who was trying to sleep at that hour could suck my left nut. The man in front of me gripped the sheets; his fists balled up as he pushed his face further and further into the pillow. The sound of his moans filling the room made me even harder, stroking my ego in all the right ways.

"You like that, don't you?" I growled, a smirk forming on my lips. "Such a needy little bitch."

I wasn't sure if his moans were involuntary or confirmation, but I took it as the latter. The more he made noise, the more it turned me on. I felt his hole tense, his body shaking under my grasp. The friction doubled between us, and I reached down, grabbing a fist full of his hair and pulling him backward. His moans doubled in volume, the pillow no longer stifling him. His back arched gracefully as my thick cock plunged into his hole over and over again. I could feel my own orgasm building at last, my thrusts growing erratic as I neared the edge.

But before I got there, the courtesan cried out, thick ropes of cum splashing over the bed linens as he came involuntarily. His hole pulsed around my shaft, driving me over the edge at last. My abs tensed as my balls drew up, and with one final thrust, I slammed my cock home, filling his guts with my seed. Wave after wave of pleasure filled my body, each as little smaller than the last as I emptied my balls at last.

With a final sigh, I slipped out of him, letting him collapse on the bed in a heap of sweat, cum, and sex. I took a step back, leaning against the foot of the bed to look at my handiwork. If there was one thing that I liked more than anything, it was seeing how I left men shaking after having my way with them. Reaching down, I scooped up a towel hanging over the bedframe and wiped myself down. I'd grab a bath later once I got back. But right now, I needed to move. The magic keeping me in human form would fade soon, and I didn't want to get caught without it. I could only do it once a day for an hour or so, and I was fairly certain I had only minutes left.

However, no sooner had the thought entered my mind than I felt the shift begin. Glancing down, I watched as the half-hard cock I was wiping off with the towel thickened, the base of the shaft thickening into a wide knot and turning black before fading to red as it neared the tip. Ridges and scaly skin covered it, and I felt the long line of rounded nubs on the underside form once more. My hands had a similar coloration, the scales and claws forming. Even my clothes shifted to accommodate my much larger dragon form. I remained humanoid in shape, but as I glanced in the mirror, I saw the long snout, horns, and spines that marked me as the *monster* I was.

And, of course, that was the moment the courtesan decided to turn around.

His eyes grew wide, his mouth open in a silent scream as he tried to find his voice. I dropped the towel, placing my palm over his lips and pressing him to the bed before he could cry out. The fear in his expression was delicious, but I didn't want it to bring the entire city of Bourveil down upon me.

"Be quiet, or I'll make sure you're quiet forever, got it?" I hissed, my voice nearly an octave lower than it had been a moment ago. "You provided me a service, and I plan to pay you for it. Do you understand?"

I could feel his hot breath against my hand and nearly *hear* his racing heart in his chest. The man was scared for his life. And, I supposed, he should have been. It wasn't every day that someone came face to face with the Beast of Bourveil Thicket and lived to tell the tale.

"Look, here's your money," I said, reaching into my pouch and producing five gold coins. "More than three times what we agreed on." I tossed it to the bed, the metal jangling as it landed on the sheets next to him. "Keep quiet, and I will leave peacefully, okay?"

Slowly I removed my hand, making sure not to pull it too far away at first. He didn't scream immediately, and I began to relax, giving him a little more space.

"See?" I said. "No harm done."

"B-but didn't you k-kill all those m-men l-last winter?" the courtesan stuttered.

"Sure did," I replied, slipping my dragon cock away and buttoning up my pants. "That's what happens when you enter my home without asking."

"And b-burned the f-farms?"

"Oh, that was just for fun," I smiled, exposing my rows of sharp fangs. "Sometimes I get the itch to start a fire now and then." I finished buckling my belt and placed both my hands on the bed, leaning down close to him. "Sometimes, I sneak into town and steal things. And sometimes those things are people..." I traced a thick black claw across his cheek. "Especially delicious little morsels like *you*."

I felt him shudder under my touch, and I couldn't help but smile.

"W-will I... Will I become a m-monster t-too?"

I couldn't help but laugh. "Maybe," I replied, giving him a small wink. "You're filled with enough dragon cum to turn any man into a beast." I watched his eyes grow even wider. "But I think you'll be okay. It's not a blue moon tonight, and that's the only time the curse can be transferred."

Watching his emotions run the gamut was deeply entertaining as I fed him lie after lie. I'd been going to town for sex for years, and not a single one of them had turned into dragon shifters. But, every single one that had seen my true form asked the same damn questions. It was almost starting to get boring.

"Well, I have to go," I said, breaking the tension between us. Leaning down, I placed a rough, scaly kiss on his cheek. "Maybe I'll see you again. I know your scent now, and you'll be easy to find."

With a dramatic swish of my long leather coat, I turned to the window, threw it open, and jumped two stories down to the alleyway below. It was an easy jump, nothing my body couldn't handle. But the moment my feet hit the dirt, I pulled my hood up, trying to cover my face as much as possible.

Most days, I could pass as a Draak, the majority of people seeing the horns wrote me off immediately. The problem was the extra features. Draak looked mostly human except for their horns and patches of scales here and there. They didn't have long snouts, giant fangs, spines, and a long tail like the one I had curled up under my coat. Not to mention, people didn't like them much, to begin with. Dragons, on the other hand, were despised on a universal level. From childhood, everyone was taught to fear and hate those great monsters of the past. Anyone that looked remotely similar was quickly shunned and usually killed. The only reason dragons persisted was because of their ability to mask themselves as humans for long periods of time.

A gift that I didn't possess.

And thanks to my parents deciding to die and orphan me at a young age, I hadn't been taught how to control my dragon half. The

Brotherhood was the only reason I'd survived until now, but I'd left them behind years ago to be on my own. I was better off without them. Besides, they probably wouldn't like what I'd been up to anyway.

At the edge of the alley, I pressed my back against the wall, getting a good look at the streets before I made my move. I'd have to keep to the shadows if I wanted to stay out of sight, but in the middle of the afternoon, that was a tall order. Still, it wasn't like I could just sit there all day, waiting for the sun to go down.

The moment the streets were clear, I took a deep breath and stepped out into the light, keeping my head down as I briskly headed for the north side of town.

"There he is!" I heard a familiar voice behind me call. "That's the beast!"

I glanced back. It was the courtesan from the tavern, and he was speaking with a pair of guards, his finger pointed in my direction. Hadn't I given him enough gold to keep his fucking mouth shut? In hindsight, maybe I'd been too nice. I should have just killed him the moment he saw me. The other times I'd been seen had just blossomed into rumors. Never before had I been called out to the guards less than five minutes later.

"Hey you!" one of the guards cried. "Stop!"

"Fuck..." I muttered under my breath, digging my boots into the dirt to pick up speed.

"STOP!"

The sound of boots crunching against the gravel told me that the guards weren't going to give up easily. I really didn't want to fight anyone, especially after such a good orgasm, but I had a feeling I was going to have to get a little dramatic if I wanted to get out of town alive. However, I'd try to outrun them first.

Or at least that's what I thought.

The twang of a bowstring was all the warning I got before an arrow slammed into the back of my shoulder. The metal tip bit into my flesh, pushing through the muscle and out the other side. I cried out, skidding to a halt as the blood began to drip down my coat. I glanced down at the wound, hissing between my teeth.

"You... You ruined my favorite coat!" I snarled at the guards as they came to a stop in front of me. I reached up and snapped the shaft of the arrow, pulling it completely through so that the wound bled freely. "You're going to fucking *pay* for that..."

Pulling my hood back, I revealed my face and horns, letting the bright sunlight soak into my scaly skin. I couldn't help but smirk as both the guard's faces went white as a sheet in a matter of seconds. The one with the bow already had another arrow nocked and although his grip was shaky, he was pointing it right at me. But this time, I knew it was coming.

A second later, the bowstring twanged again, the arrow streaking through the air straight toward my heart. With a lazy flick of my hand, I conjured a shimmering magical shield around my entire body, the arrow skipping off harmlessly.

"This is your last warning," I growled, holding my ground. "Either let me pass in peace or forfeit your lives."

The guards glanced at one another; their eyes full of fear. The one with the bow pulled another arrow while the other clutched his sword with white knuckles.

"In the n-name of the Tide Fighters, y-you are under a-arrest," the bowman shuddered. "Come q-quietly or b-be put d-down!"

"Oh, you poor dumb thing," I sighed, shaking my head. "You stand no chance against the Beast of Bourveil Thicket."

The bowman's hands were shaking as he stared at me, his eyes wide with fear. I continued to stare them down, my hands laced in front of me. All I needed them to do was put down their weapons and I'd walk away without issue. Although, if I was being honest, I kind of wanted them to come after me. I'd been itching for a while to blow off some steam and taking out a couple of Tide Fighters really jived with me. I had enough magic left in me to protect myself and get away, that much I was sure of. However, should they manage to call reinforcements, I might be in a little bit of trouble.

"Just walk away," I hissed. "If you value your lives that is."

The one with the sword jabbed it toward me, shouting much louder than necessary. "The Tide Fighters d-don't back down from b-beasts like you!"

I couldn't help but smirk. "Have it your way then."

The moment the words left my lips, there was another twang of a bowstring. I didn't even flinch as the arrow ricocheted off the magic shield surrounding me. The smirk on my face widened as I stared them down, a low chuckle in my throat.

It was time to play.

"Big mistake," I snarled, digging the balls of my feet into the dirt.

With a gust of wind, the back of my coat was thrown wide, massive draconic wings unfurling behind me. It wasn't often that people got to see them and judging by the expressions of horror on the guard's faces, they hadn't been expecting it. I dug the balls of my feet into the gravel, launching myself forward before either of them could react.

In a flash the sword was knocked free of the one on the right. I grabbed him by the throat and pulled him close, crushing his windpipe within my grasp. He clawed at my hand, his legs flailing uselessly as he tried to get himself free. I could see the tears forming in his eyes as he stared up at me, his face growing more and more red as my grip tightened.

"You should have left while you had the chance," I whispered.

With a simple jerk of my wrist I felt his neck snap and his body went limp. I tossed him easily to the side where he landed in a heap, no longer a part of Eadronem or the turning of the sun. My gaze shifted to the other who was fumbling with his bow, trying desperately to nock another arrow even though the last two had failed spectacularly. I guess he didn't quite get the picture either.

Effortlessly I stepped forward and grabbed the bow, crushing the wood in my hands. With the other I slipped my fingers under his armor, jerking his body close so we were face to face. I tossed the broken bow to the side and reached up, caressing his cheek with the back of a claw.

"A kiss before you go, I think," I smiled, taking a deep breath.

He didn't get a chance to react before I forced our lips together. For a moment I stared into his eyes, relishing in the mixture of fear and confusion that crossed his features. Then I closed my eyes, slowly breathing out into his mouth. His body tensed in my grasp and he struggled for a moment before going still. The smell of smoke and burning hair met my nostrils, but I didn't stop. They'd tried to kill me and I was going to enjoy my fun. It wasn't like I got to vent my frustrations like that very often.

It wasn't until the breath had completely left my body that I finally pulled away. My eyes fluttered open, my gaze falling on the charred corpse smoldering within his own armor in front of me. In his open mouth I could see the dull glow of embers, the interior of his body still burning from my dragon breath. The heat licked at my skin, but I felt no pain. I was immune to fire. But he wasn't.

With a small chuckle, I let go of his armor, the body striking the gravel and breaking into several glowing embers. Sparks rose in the air as I stretched my wings, kicking up a bit of wind in the process. I felt satisfied with the day's work I'd accomplished. My ears perked up as I caught the sound of soldiers heading my direction. They'd be really pissed once they found their comrades dead in the street. Even if I wanted to fight more, they'd probably overwhelm me. It was time to go home. I'd come back for the courtesan another time.

Turning away from the smoldering corpse, I began to run up the street to the north. A few heavy flaps of my massive wings was all it took to catch the breeze, lifting me off my feet. Within a few seconds I was airborne, rising above the low buildings of Bourveil and into the sky. A quick glance back showed the soldiers converging on the street where we'd fought, their cries reaching my ears as they pointed up to the sky.

Maybe they'd remember that next time one of them dared to tangle with the Beast of Bourveil Thicket.

***

Grab your copy of Dragon's Redemption now! ⇨ https://a.co/d/8ylDPNm

Don't miss out!

Visit the website below and you can sign up to receive emails whenever Blake R. Wolfe publishes a new book. There's no charge and no obligation.

https://books2read.com/r/B-A-CVCS-KVDKC

BOOKS 2 READ

Connecting independent readers to independent writers.

Also by Blake R. Wolfe

Bone, Stone, and Wood
Exordium
Arbitrium
Profundum
The Crystal Moon

Tales of the Tellurian Pack
Alpha's Rejection
Beta's Bliss
Gamma's Dive
Omega's Folly

The Crystalline Chronicles
The Crystal Eye
The Crystal Archivist
The Crystal Key
The Crystal Heart

The Shifter Brotherhood
Wolf's Blessing

The Tales of Bramoria
The Grimoire of Kings
The Sage and the Phoenix
The Crown of Madness

Standalone
Jonathan's Letter
Lake Arcadia

Watch for more at https://www.blakerwolfe.com.

About the Author

Blake spends most nights with his laptop pulled close, clacking away on the keyboard to get the next great idea written down. Surrounded by piles of notebooks, journals, and a cat of course, he does his best to keep his brain on the task at hand.

Blake has published across multiple genres, but prefers the fantasy realm to all others. He is a beach bum during the summer, a wannabe yogi, and an avid Muppets fan. Seriously.

You can sign up for new releases, giveaways, and freebies on his website.

Read more at https://www.blakerwolfe.com.

Milton Keynes UK
Ingram Content Group UK Ltd.
UKHW010743180923
428890UK00001B/66